PAINTINGS
FROM THE
CAVE

ALSO BY GARY PAULSEN

GARY PAULSEN

PAINTINGS FROM THE CAVE

THREE NOVELLAS

WENDY
L A M B
BOOKS

30531 2256

A

Text copyright © 2011 by Gary Paulsen
Jacket art copyright © 2011 by Andy Smith

Visit us on the Web! www.randomhouse.com/teens
Educators and librarians, for a variety of teaching tools, visit us at
www.randomhouse.com/teachers

Library of Congress Cataloging-in-Publication Data
Paulsen, Gary.
   Paintings from the cave : three novellas / Gary Paulsen. — 1st ed.
      p.   cm.
   Summary: "In these three novellas, Gary Paulsen explores how children can survive the most difficult circumstances through art and the love of dogs"— Provided by publisher.
   Contents: Man of the iron heads — Jo-Jo the dog-faced girl — Erik's rules.
   ISBN 978-0-385-74684-7 (trade) — ISBN 978-0-385-90921-1 (lib. bdg.) — ISBN 978-0-375-89743-6 (ebook) — ISBN 978-0-553-49466-2 (pbk.)
   [1. Short stories. 2. Violence—Fiction. 3. Homeless persons—Fiction. 4. Art—Fiction. 5. Dogs—Fiction.]   I. Title.
   PZ7.P2843Pai 2011   [Fic]—dc23   2011016287

Printed in the United States of America
10 9 8 7 6 5 4 3 2 1
First Edition

This book is for
my friends
Teri Lesesne and Kylene Beers—
and every teacher and librarian like them—
who work tirelessly to put books
in the hands of young readers.
Thank you.

CONTENTS

A NOTE FROM THE AUTHOR

I was one of the kids who slipped through the cracks. I had what is euphemistically referred to as a troubled childhood.

We were broke, my parents were drunks, they had—another euphemism here—an unhappy marriage. I was an outsider at school and I pretty much raised myself at home. I had nothing and I was going nowhere.

But then art and dogs saved me.

First reading, then writing. First friend-pets, then sled dogs. They gave me hope that I wouldn't always be stuck in the horror of my childhood, made me believe that there could be more to my life.

Over the years since I've been writing books, I've met thousands of kids, either in person or by letter, and it's not uncommon for young people to confide in me about the nightmare of their home lives, because I've always been so open about my own.

One time, though, in Topeka, Kansas, when I was visiting my friend the librarian Mike Printz and talking about my childhood to a bunch of kids in his library, a girl raised her hand and, in a flat, quiet voice, asked me, "But what do you do when it's bad? When it gets really, really bad?"

I remember wondering what I could possibly say to her that would make a difference to her right then and there. Because, somehow, "Someday things will get better, someday you'll be old enough to leave home, someday you can put this behind you, someday all of this will feel like it's a million miles away . . ." didn't seem authentic enough to match the honesty of her question.

Because someday, to that girl, *was* a million miles away. She had the here and now to deal with. As so many do. So many heres and nows that are cold and ugly and raw and cruel and vicious, with little to no hope.

As I looked at her across the library, I saw so many faces of kids who believed themselves to be rejected and abandoned, unloved and unlovable.

And so to Jake and Jo and Jamie—three kids in (another euphemism here) unstable environments with nothing and no one to protect and raise them. Except for dogs and art and that little hot worm deep inside us all that, no matter how damaged and broken we are, still allows us to respond to the beauty that art provides or the love that a good dog gives.

MAN OF THE
IRON HEADS

Sometimes you move right, sometimes left, in the dark, out of the light, always moving.

You stop moving, you're done.

My name is Jake 'cept they call me just J in the building. My aunt, she lives on eighteen, door 1872. I've been with her since my ma . . . went away when I was three, maybe four. So I guess you could call that home, 'cept she looks right through me most of the time, calls me trouble, nothing but trouble, born trouble, so I haven't really lived in 1872 since I was seven. She never wanted to get stuck with a kid, she tells me, so everything I do that makes her remember I'm around is trouble in her eyes. So I stay away as much as I can, sleep on the couch at Layla's every night because her ma's either sleeping or working. That's all she does, all she has time to do, she says. Sleep and work, two shifts, every day. I hide in the basement in the day. Stay low.

I'm either eleven or twelve years old now; I lost track and my aunt doesn't care enough to keep it straight. The school probably has papers on me, they're big on forms and being official, but it doesn't really matter how old I am. I learned a long time ago that the only thing that matters is that I gotta keep moving.

You stop, you're done.

You stop, Blade gets you.

They call him Blade because he used a knife on a boy one time—cut a notch in his tongue—marked him so everybody knows he talked back to Blade one too many times. But he doesn't use a knife anymore. Not since he got a Glock Nine with a staggered clip, holds more bullets than God made.

They say he busted a cap in Fat Charlie's gut just to see what would happen.

Made a big hole, that's what happened.

They say Charlie didn't do nothing but laugh at the wrong time, but I think there's more to it than that. Doesn't matter the reason, though, 'cause—bang— Charlie's shot. They say Blade watched Charlie bleed, just stood there, watching, didn't leave until he heard the sirens coming.

Blade stays clear of sirens because he's in business.

Blade sells it all, highs and lows, weed and pills and

powder, sells guns, sells people if they don't keep moving.

So I move left, right, in the dark, out of the light, moving.

I was moving away from Blade when I found the man with the iron heads.

2

$\mathbf{B}$lade's boys are always on the street in front of the apartment building and hanging around the front door because Blade is in 1604 selling through a little hole in a steel door. His boys watch for the cops.

I watch for them. I watch for Blade's boys every waking minute of every day. I open my eyes in the morning, I look for Blade's boys. I close my eyes at night, last thing I look for is Blade's boys.

When I see them run up the front stairs, where they trade Blade a wad of cash for what he sells, then I make my move.

Just inside the building, next to the old chipped back door, is the super's door to the basement. But the super doesn't come around much anymore, not since Blade started running the building. And the super never goes in the basement, not since Blade got his Glock.

The lock to the basement door doesn't work, even though the door sticks, so I lift the handle, kick the bottom, push the door open. Then I slip down the stairwell to the warm and dirty furnace room.

I hear rats as big as ponies moving in the far corners, but they run away as I creep the length of the basement to a window. Then I climb up and out into the empty lot in the back where it's dark, no streetlights shine back there.

Forty steps and I'm at the basement window of the next building.

Empty now because they say they're gonna do something called urban renewal. Never happens, though, and now the building stinks from the winos and the junkies. They're no worry to me—they stay in the front of the building where the sun sometimes shines and warms them, because it's January, ice everywhere. There are rats running around, hiding in the piles of garbage that were left behind when everyone moved out and left the building to fall apart, but I got a stick if they get too close. Big stick.

But the back of the building is where I've got my place to be when I'm too tired or cold to keep moving. I look out those back windows, or holes where the windows were, and I can see into the building on the other side of the alley.

Clean.

Warm.

Light.

Bright.

New.

Rich.

Just ten steps away, the good life. No rats, no Glock Nines, no druggies shaking and crying and puking. Just ten steps away, but it might as well be a whole 'nother world.

Layla didn't believe me when I first told her about this place. She could still get around then, back when she wasn't so far along like she is now, so I brought her here.

She was fourteen, not quite fifteen, when one of Blade's men caught her. Around here, like I said, you gotta keep moving.

But Layla didn't keep moving.

We don't talk about that, I probably wouldn't have even known if she hadn't started getting big.

A few months ago, when the construction noise ended and the tenants moved into the apartments, I brought her into this building to look across the alley at the new-old building.

"See?" I pointed.

Rich folks buy old buildings, fix them up, make

apartments they call lofts. Then they put up a fence to keep us out. Wire leans our way at the top, razor rippers so we can't get over them.

We can see through the fence, though.

Layla and I could see the people through the windows. We watched a party in one apartment. Counted the people who came with packages, shiny paper on big-ass boxes. Saw the cake and the candles. Heard the singing.

No one ever sang to me or Layla.

I just brought Layla the one time because pretty soon she was too far along that she couldn't get through the basement window anymore.

I still come because I've got to have my place to be and none of Blade's boys think to come back here. No business, no reason for them to be here.

I sit in the basement and look out the windows. It's freezing cold, not like the furnace room in my building, where it's warm. That's where I used to spend most days, but I couldn't see anything in the furnace room 'cept rats and shadows. Here I can see into six apartments across the alley.

I see two men who live in the same apartment on the fourth floor yelling at each other. One of them throws a plate at the wall and the other one slams a door. Just like our side of the block. Only, later I see them laughing when they sweep up the broken plate together.

Fifth floor, a mother and her daughter, she looks

about Layla's age. They hug a lot—hello, goodbye, good night—laugh, eat breakfast and supper together. It's sweet. Things'd be different if Layla's ma had time to treat her like that.

Then I see the man with the iron heads.

Middle right, over to the side, closest to where I watch, and he has four windows so I can see his loft the best. It's smaller than the others. He wears old clothes and he seems young, too young to have a place like that, on his own even, but rich people are different. One window is the kitchen and he stands over the sink and eats fast out of a pot like he doesn't care what he's eating. He's looking into the other room the whole time he eats.

I can see better if I move and so I go into the next room and look out the window into his other room.

I see heads.

Not real ones, but three, no four, made of something gray, like mud, placed on skinny little tall tables around the room.

He's making heads.

When I get cold, it's time to go back up to Layla's. I don't like her to be on her own for too long these days. And I never want her to be alone when it gets dark and her ma's working night shifts.

But I don't move.

Not sure why. My knees are stiff with the cold and even my Eskimo coat with the fur around my face can't keep me warm. Course, it's got holes, from before I found it in the Dumpster.

My coat keeps me pretty warm even though it gets so cold that steam comes from the grates. When the steam comes up into the street, there could be bodies in the morning. The worst night, three dead winos were froze so stiff the emergency guys couldn't unbend them. They took the bodies away still crooked.

I should go, but I don't.

There's something about the heads.

They look alive.

The man sets the pot in the sink and moves into the room with the heads. As he starts working on one with his hands, pushing the mud this way and that, it looks even more alive.

He keeps looking back in a corner where I can't see unless I go up a floor but that's too far because I'd have to go toward the front of the building, then up, then back. The crackheads are there. It's not so hard to get past them, but it takes time, and you never know, one of Blade's people might be there so it's not worth the risk.

But still, I don't leave.

I can't see what he's looking at but I watch his hands and the way he keeps looking up and then back at the head. He's frowning but somehow he's happy, too. I don't know how I know that, I just know.

Finally I can't stand the cold and, just as I get up to go, he bumps one of the stands and a head falls to the floor.

Clunk.

I can hear the sound through his closed window, ten feet across the alley, and through the broken window where I'm crouching.

That head isn't made of mud, but of something metal.

He makes iron heads, he sits in his kitchen eating from a pot staring at heads he makes of mud and iron.

I'm so cold now my teeth are chattering. It's late, too. If I don't get back up to Layla's apartment soon, I'll run into Blade's people. If they're out and about, I'm in. Somewhere, anywhere, doesn't matter, just so that I'm not where they can see me.

Still, it's hard to leave and I lean closer to see a little more before I have to go.

The man sees me.

He turns, and there we are.

Eye to eye. Ten steps away.

And he smiles. Nods and smiles to say hi, so I raise my hand, kinda wave back at him.

Then I turn away to go tell Layla about the man with the iron heads.

We talk about everything together. Everything except how she got that big belly. And I know she'll think I'm making this up. Sometimes I do make things up, to get her to laugh, so I gotta make sure I tell this straight so she understands, so she knows, so she can see what I see—a man across the alley making metal heads out of mud in his living room.

But first, I got to get to the other side of the basement, across the alley, through the other window, past the furnace, then wait, wait, wait . . .

Okay. Now up the back stairs that smell like pee so bad you can't breathe. Fast. Quiet. Looking around the whole time. No one sees me. I don't see no one. I like it that way.

Finally to Layla's door on the twelfth floor. Door 1240.

I gotta keep moving.

'Cause you stop, you're done.

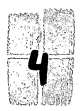

A man came to school once, back when I still went to school kind of regular. Now I hardly go at all. 'Cause I got to keep moving and they don't go for that in school, they make you stay put.

So this guy, he wrote a book and he talked like we read books.

Like we *got* books.

He talked about chapters and what he did to tell the story and then he asked if there were any questions. What were *we* gonna ask *him*? Nobody stuck their hand up but me.

I put up my hand because I had two things I wanted to know about this man who wrote books and thought we should read them and talk with him about them.

"You ever been bitten by a rat?"

He got real quiet. I kept talking.

"Sharp teeth, rats. Alley rats run, but basement rats don't always run. Sometimes they stand still and you can kill them with a stick or a brick. They got teeth like razors."

I thought the man wasn't gonna say anything. Finally he said no. "A dog bit me once, but it wasn't bad, he bit me on the ankle and then ran away."

Then I showed him marks on *my* ankle where the rats bit me and he looked like he was going to cry. From seeing rat marks. He should have seen the dead wino frozen to a grate, bits of his face left there when they dragged him off. So rat bites don't mean anything.

I asked him the second question.

"They made us read that book you wrote and everybody in your book was happy, living in good houses, talking about their problems until the problems went away. Course, they didn't have no one screaming on the street corner all night long, they didn't have drunks asleep in their hallways in puddles of pee first thing in the morning, those people in your book. But anyway, in this book you wrote—there was a mother who cooked and cleaned and a father who went to work every day and came home every day and a big brother who didn't smack anyone around—is that true?"

He looked at the clock, shoved his hands in his pockets, looked down at the floor—not at me, not at anyone else in the room, either—cleared his throat and said, "Yes. There are families like that."

"From around here?"

He nodded. "Many of them."

Then we knew he was lying.

I quit going to school regular when I found out they were lying to us.

Besides, there's more to learning than what's in school.

Just getting through a day takes a whole world of knowing.

5

It's not so bad early in the day.

Blade, he's a night man. What he sells doesn't move in the morning.

First thing in the morning—food.

I check the fridges. Layla's ma buys week-old bread and lunch meat. When she thinks of it, my aunt buys big cans of beans.

I eat lunch meat and bread and beans till I just about puke.

I'm still hungry after the beans are gone, though. Cans are big, but not that big, and nothing lasts forever.

I used to shop for food at Skinny Tony's corner store half a block away. I used to shop without money, but Skinny Tony got too smart. He brought in an old hockey stick. He catches you taking something, you get the hockey stick so hard it makes your ears ring.

I don't shop at Skinny Tony's without money anymore.

Guys used to come with guns and rob him, too. But Skinny Tony got his own Glock Nine. A crackhead came in with a little .22 peashooter pistol and Skinny Tony blasted him to pieces.

So no one tries to rob Skinny Tony anymore.

The best way to get money is to wait until the monthly checks come and everybody's messed up. Then I sweep their pockets or purses for change. After I hit up Layla's ma and my aunt, I'll go through some other apartments where the locks don't work right. I mostly get small bills. Now and then a ten. Once a twenty. Sometimes just change. Doesn't matter; I take what I can find.

I used to work the street, go two, three blocks away, where no one knew me, and hold my hand out.

I don't do that anymore.

Because out there I'm an easy target. Blade or his boys, they come by and I'm done. Got to keep moving. You stop moving, you're done.

If you don't take money from pockets and purses in the building and you won't stand on the streets, another way to get money for food in my building is to work for Blade. I've seen it happen to enough people. I know how it works.

He has them stand on a corner, and when the cops come, the people call Blade on a cell. At first he pays them with money, maybe some new shoes. They think things are good. Then he says it's time to sell some weed. Okay, no big deal, weed is chump change around here. Then the weed turns into something else. They're still doing fine until the day comes when they stop selling, start using. And that day always comes.

Then they're done. Finished.

Because Blade's inside their heads then. He owns them and they have to sell more and more to keep up, and pretty soon he's selling *them.*

Boy, girl, it doesn't matter. There are people who buy both. There are always new kids to catch, kids who don't keep moving, don't know the safe places to be, think they can sell and not be sold.

Now, even without money I still got to eat.

Today I make a mistake and try to lift something at Skinny Tony's. I catch the hockey stick. When I run out of the store I'm not watching, and I stop and hold my head.

You stop, you're done.

Blade gets me.

6

Course it isn't Blade, but one of his people. Blade doesn't have to leave the building. His people bring him food, women, all the things he sells. And money. Blade has guys who beat the crap out of whoever gets on his bad side so he doesn't have to go do it himself. Today that's me.

Petey catches me. They call him that because he drinks Sneaky Pete—cheap wine.

Petey grabs my wrist with his sharp hands that're like big claws. Strong for such a skinny man.

"J. How you be?"

I pull left and right but he's got me. For now. Cold.

"I'm chillin'," I say. "Stayin' out of trouble."

"How's that girl? What's her name? Layla?"

"I don't know," I lie. "I never see her. Guess she's okay."

"She's fine, just fine. Blade wants to see her after she has her brat. She'll be gettin' a monthly check then. Blade wants to see her. 'Bout that check, 'bout some other things."

"What's that to me?"

"I know you talk to her. You tell her that after she has the kid, Blade wants to see her."

I wait for his grip to loosen, but it stays tight.

"Blade wants to talk to you, too."

"I got nothing he wants."

"You got you. That's what Blade wants to see you about."

"What's he want me for?" I know the answer but I'm stalling, hoping Petey's grip will loosen. He's a little drunk, a little high, but he's moving down, not up, and he'll be nodding out soon.

"Blade is always looking for new . . . opportunities. . . ."

It's a big word for him, and he has to think, slow down. His hand loosens and I'm gone.

He swears after me but I'm clean down the alley. Nobody can catch me now because I'm fast and quiet. I run like flying birds. Alley wind. God's alley wind. I run all the way to the corner before I look back to see him trying to run after me and stumbling.

I go right, down Second Street, but not too far away

from what I know. The only thing worse than being on Blade's street is when you find yourself on someone else's. Someone you don't know, someone who doesn't know you, someone with a whole new set of rules, someone who's just like Blade but might even be worse, might leave his building, might take care of things himself, not send some skinny dumb drunk you can get away from quick.

One block, clean, then into the alley on the next block. I stop and look back but Petey isn't even out of the first alley, so I double back, slowing down, running from Dumpster to Dumpster, keeping the garbage between me and anybody looking for me.

Pretty soon I'm back behind my own building, looking over to the busted basement window of the empty building where I've got my place.

Nobody's around so I truck across the lot and slide down through the window into the basement. Finally, I'm in my place, watching the other world.

People are eating dinner. I'd forgotten how hungry I was, but now I remember and I can almost touch the smell of food. My stomach growls as I watch. Seems everyone in that building eats at the same time. Must be something rich folks do, eat at the same time every day. Together.

Iron-head man is gone, his four windows are dark, so I lean back and wait. I can't go out for a while. Petey's maybe waiting to catch me again—if he can even remember. If he does, though, he'll be mad and might make it worse than the first time. So I have to stay put. I chill, which is true 'cause it's cold.

In a few minutes the iron-head man comes back. He throws his coat over a chair in the kitchen, pulls a pan from the fridge and puts it in the oven. Then he goes into the room with the heads and starts working.

He's pinching at the mud with his thumbs and then looking in the corner where I can't see. He looks across the room while he lets his fingers trace the head he's working on.

I decide to move up a floor so I'll be even with him because I've gotta see back in that corner. When I watch that man touch the mud, I forget where I am. When I see those heads, I'm not cold and hungry, standing in a filthy dump anymore. This is the one place where I can see something beautiful and where I feel warm on the inside.

When I get upstairs, I look out from this new window and there he is. But I still can't see enough. So I go one room over, chase a rat out, and then I can finally see in that corner.

He's got a picture of a man leaning against a chair. It's a big one, like a poster. But he's just making the head of the man.

All of a sudden the kitchen's full of smoke and he

runs to take the pan out of the oven. He drops it in the sink, opens the window and swears some good blue words. I can hear what he says because there's no glass in my window and we can't be more than ten feet apart.

He looks up from the sink and sees me standing there, watching him. We're staring right at each other, so close that I can see that his eyes are sparkly, but not shiny like he's lost to something Blade sells. He's got black skin, and he's . . . bright, somehow, like there's a streetlight shining out from his insides right through his skin, right over to me.

He's bald and his head gleams like he polished it. I'm surprised that he's so young. I'm not good at guessing ages—it doesn't matter much how old you are where I live, but he doesn't seem old enough to have a place on his own. Not one that nice, anyway.

"Hello," he says. "I saw you the other day. I'm Bill."

I nod, but I don't say anything. He waits a minute and then says, "What's your name?"

"Jake. But everybody calls me J. Just the letter."

"Well, J-just-the-letter, I'd invite you to dinner, but as you can see I pretty much burned the life out of it."

Yeah, I think. Offering me food. Right. Across a fence. Put it on a stick, hold it out in the air. Like feeding something at a zoo. I saw a man on the TV once, feeding crocodiles meat on the end of a stick so that he didn't have to get close.

"I'm not hungry. Much."

He looks at me for a long time. Not in a bad way, but like he's figuring me out. "How about I order a pizza?"

I stare at him, saying nothing.

"Don't you like pizza?"

"You want to eat pizza with me?"

"Sure."

"Across a fence."

"Fence?" He looks out and down like he just noticed we're talking across an alley. "Well, no. You'll have to come over here. I'll let you in the building."

Pizza sounds good, but I know that some people are bad to the bone when they see a kid. Blade sells to people like that. I've seen it happen.

This guy doesn't seem like one of them. But I know that bad people don't always look different on the outside. People can look good, be bad—it's all in their heads.

"Why're you doin' this?" I ask.

"Inviting you to split a pizza with me?"

"Yeah."

"You have a good face."

I shake my head. Look away.

"What?"

"I'm not one of those boys like on the street. . . ."

"You think I'm somebody who would . . . *bother* a child?" His face looks like that writer guy from school when I asked if he knew about rat bites. Kinda like he's frozen or something.

"I'm not a child. I'm el . . . twelve. No one asks someone to come over for pizza without a reason."

He exhales, rubs the back of his neck. "Well, J, I do have a reason for inviting you over for pizza: I'd like to make a few studies of you, your face and your head."

"What for?"

"I'm a sculptor. I'm making three-dimensional images of figures—right now it's just heads—in clay. And I'd like you to sit on a stool here in my studio so I could sketch the lines and planes and curves of your head in clay to sculpt later."

"Why would I do that?"

"Because I'll pay you. Pizza and ten dollars."

"Ten dollars to sit and eat pizza?"

"Yeah."

"That's it? You won't touch me?"

"God, no. I promise."

Then I think I have him. "You want me to take my clothes off?" I saw that on TV once, an artist made pictures of naked people. I don't have no truck with that.

"No. Not at all. I just want to look at your head. I'm doing a study of heads right now and I realize, looking at you, that all I've done are adult figures. I'd like to try to capture a young person's form."

I don't know what he's talking about. But he's got food and he's got money. And I can give them both to Layla afterwards. She likes pizza and she needs the money. I can do this for Layla. Besides, I want to see the heads.

"All right. Where do I go?"

He smiles again. "Go to the next block." He points out the window to the front of his building. "I'll meet you there."

So I go to the basement, out the window, down the alley to the street that runs alongside the building, looking for Petey all the way. But I never go this way, so it's not likely Petey does, either.

I walk along the fence on the side street, to the front of the iron-head man's building. He's there and he opens the door and holds out his hand.

"What's that for?" I ask.

"To shake."

"I told you: no touching."

He nods and moves back so I can step through the door.

I slip past him. And I go into Bill's world.

7

Once when I was still in school, they took us on a trip downtown to the library and a museum where a bunch of dead people's things were laid out for us to look at.

Those places were like Bill's world.

Quiet. Clean. Warm.

His hallway doesn't smell of pee and worse, and the walls are clean, no gangbanger raps spray-painted everywhere.

He waits for me to go ahead of him, but I tip my head at him so that he'll walk in front of me and I can keep an eye on him. I got to keep moving and I got to watch things. A person could get in trouble if he doesn't do that.

The elevator works. The place doesn't stink and the

elevator works. I shake my head. We go up to his floor and down the hall to his loft.

He's got no real rooms like the apartments I know, it's one big space. The kitchen is at one end and I see his bed, just a piece of foam and a blanket, in a corner. A couch that's missing a cushion is under the windows and he's got piles of books everywhere—so many that it looks like that library they took us to. I wonder how long it took this man to read all these books. No TV, but soft sounds coming from a radio. It's not really music 'cause there isn't any real punch to it. The wood floors are clean and shiny. Not like the torn carpets in my building, so old they aren't even a color anymore.

His place smells funny. Like burned food from the oven, then paint, and something from the statues.

Statues.

From the windows I could only see three or four of them. Inside, I see that statues are all over, some small, some a little bigger. Not all of them are heads. One statue is a bird with open wings and there are a few small statues of girls dancing, little arms out like they're spinning around so you think they're moving.

I look at the pictures on all the walls and a wooden frame with a big white pad of paper in one corner of the big room.

Off to the side is a bathroom. I take a quick peek: clean. Just to make sure, I flush the toilet.

He's watching me, so I say, "We don't even have water half the time."

He looks out the window, across the fence. "That's not right."

No shit, I think. That's not right. There's nothing right about the other side of the fence. Everything's different over there. Even the air.

"You live here all the time?" I ask. "Is this your home, or just where you come to make heads?"

"A little of both, I guess. It's just my place to go."

"Yeah, I got one of those too. A man needs his place to go."

He looks at me, frowning, and continues, "I won a small grant. It's not much, but it's enough so that I don't have to worry about money and I was able to leave school for a while."

"Yeah, me too."

He raises an eyebrow so I say, "I left school too. Only"—I laugh through my nose—"I don't think it's for just a while."

"But . . ." He starts to say something, stares at me for a second, then looks at a number on the wall, picks up the phone and punches the buttons. "What kind of pizza do you want?"

"A big one. With everything 'cept them little stinking fish."

"Anchovies?"

"Yeah. They smell worse than the Dumpster in the summertime."

I'm talking too much. It's better to just listen. You can't learn anything talking 'cause you're just saying stuff you already know. You've got to be quiet to learn. And keep moving.

He orders pizza, then points at the stool in the corner, next to the big picture of the man. "Would you go sit on that stool, please?"

"With my coat on?"

"It's up to you. But aren't you too warm with it on?"

Cooking like a hot dog in a bun, that's how warm I am. But I want to keep it on in case I have to run. This guy talks all right, but you never know. He could buy the pizza, then pull a knife.

But I want to see how he makes those heads and he doesn't seem bad, so I take the coat off.

I keep it close, though.

"How do you want me to sit?"

"Anyway you like, as long as you're comfortable."

"Why are you making all these heads?" I sit, prop my feet on the crossbars of the stool, stay cool. "You sell them?"

He laughs. "Well, not so far. I have to find a gallery for them so that they can be shown and sold. That's next, I guess."

"You wanna know what you should do?"

He tips his head, smiles. "Sure."

"Naked ladies. You make statues of naked ladies and they'll sell a lot faster than a bunch of heads."

He laughs again, a nice laugh. "You're probably right."

I know I'm right. I saw it on TV. Two hundred years ago some man did a painting of a naked lady and somebody just sold it for two million dollars.

"How come some of the heads are made out of iron?" I ask.

"It's not iron; they're bronze castings. All of them will be made into bronze later. If I can afford it."

"Bronze. What's that?"

"It's a mixture of metals. Copper and tin. It's quite hard."

I shrug. "Same as iron to me. I dunno from copper and tin."

He reaches into a cardboard box lined with a plastic bag and scoops handfuls of mud. He plops them on a table that's covered in newspapers, makes a big lumpy ball.

"Where do you get the mud?" I point.

"It's called clay. I order it from an art-supply store and they deliver it."

I watch him work with his hands on the clay and pretty soon I see that the head is taking shape. I see eyes, see ears, see nose and lips.

It doesn't look like me, but something makes me think of me. Like I'm in the clay somewhere. Like I'm waiting to come out.

"How do you do that?"

"Do what?"

"Make me come out of that clay."

Another smile. This iron-head man smiles more than anyone I've ever seen. Nice, though, even if I'm not used to it. Usually, when I see someone's teeth, it's 'cause they're yelling.

"I always wanted to draw or paint or do some kind of art with my hands. So I went to school to learn and then I—"

A knock on the door and I jump off the stool. Only the cops knock like that.

But it's the pizza. In all my life, I never had food brought to me.

I can smell it across the room and my stomach grumbles so loud I bet Petey and Blade, wherever they are, can hear it.

Then we eat.

He takes one piece, but he's still looking at the clay head. Chew, swallow, steady eyes.

He looks back at me, but not to talk. He tilts his head, looking hard. He sets down his pizza, goes over to the stand and starts again.

It's been a long time since I had hot food and I eat one whole piece of pizza, then another. Tastes so good my jaws hurt.

Third piece, fourth, and I slow down.

I think of Layla.

"You going to eat more?" I ask him.

He shakes his head. "I'm not that hungry. Are you enjoying it?"

Am I enjoying it? Grease and cheese around my mouth, crumbs on my T-shirt, more food than I've had in six months. I've never had enough to eat—not so much that I wasn't still a little hungry around the edges.

"It's all right."

"Then take the rest with you. I've never liked cold pizza."

There's still a little over half left for Layla and that baby inside that she's feeding.

I nod. "My friend Layla likes pizza."

"Do you think she'd come with you sometime and let me sculpt her head? I could pay her like I'm paying you. Ten dollars."

I shake my head. "Hard for Layla to get around."

"Is she sick?"

I've seen her puke her guts up in the mornings, but that's just baby sick. "No. She's going to have a baby."

"Oh." He stops pushing the clay and looks off like he's studying that picture again. Only he's not looking at anything but air. "So she's much older than you?"

I nod. "She's fifteen."

"Fifteen . . ."

He stops talking then, and starts working the clay again, and I can see he has questions. I'm thinking: In his life, he doesn't always have to be moving. In this warm, soft place he has, he doesn't know anything about how you've got to keep moving.

"She was too slow," I say. "A man caught her in a stairwell."

And I tell him about her. I don't know why, but it all comes out. Layla and me and living in the building.

He looks like he's about to cry even though it wasn't him got caught in that stairwell.

He looks out the window. "Right there across that fence . . . I didn't know."

I laugh 'cept it isn't funny. He doesn't smile back at me this time, just stands there looking out the window like he's never seen that view before. I guess he hasn't. It's not the kind of thing people notice. Not if they don't have to.

He'd stopped working, but now he starts again, slow, like he's not really paying attention. I do, though. I watch how he takes bumps and smooths them, adds bumps to where it's smooth. He runs his fingers along the slopes of the head on the stand. I could watch forever.

A while later he stops to turn on some lights and I look outside. It's dark. That's not good. Layla's alone and I've got to get back in the building. Without being seen. Carrying half a pizza. After I made Petey and Blade mad at me.

"It's time for me to go," I say.

"It's not late; it's not even six yet."

"That doesn't matter. It gets dark early in the winter. Things change when it's dark."

Bill looks out the window and then back at me, nodding. "You've got a point there."

"The night people come out," I say, because he has no idea about the dark. "And they're always looking to get it over on someone."

"I can walk you home," he offers. Like he'd know what to do if Blade's boys came up on him in the dark.

"You don't belong over there," I tell him, because I got enough to worry about getting me back to my building, without thinking about him on Blade's side of the block.

"Be careful, J."

My gut starts to tighten up around all that pizza I ate 'cause I'll be lucky to make it back and I hate when I have to be lucky. Luck is nothing to count on.

I pick up the pizza.

"I gotta go now."

And I leave.

There's nowhere to go at night that's safe. Night people with night eyes are in the alleys, in the halls. They're watching and waiting.

They'll hurt you for a dollar. They'll kill you for ten dollars.

They say a woman in the building sold her baby to Blade for a seven-dollar bag of what he sells. He turned right around and sold that baby to some rich lawyer for nine hundred dollars.

Bill's building is all lit up in front. On this side of the block, nobody breaks the bulbs so they can carry on in the dark. I hate the lights when it's dark outside 'cause everybody can see you, you can't move fast in the light.

I run back to the alley between the buildings and

then stop, listen. I stay out of sight, stop, then move, stop, then move.

A little sound. I stop again. Hold my breath, crouch down. Someone digging on the other side of the Dumpster. He doesn't know I'm there, blown-out druggie doesn't know anything. I hide, part of the dark two feet away, and he shuffles past me without knowing I'm there.

Now across to the basement window, to the furnace room. Warm, but stinking. Now that I've been in Bill's room where it didn't stink, I can smell things I didn't before. I can smell myself.

I wait in back of the furnace. Then a new smell. A smell I know. A smell I love.

"Layla?"

I hear her soft breath. "That you, J?"

"Who else?"

"You smell like food."

"Pizza. Leave the light out. Come to my voice. . . ."

"There's nobody down here but us. I left the light off so nobody'd think I'm here. I've been here for over an hour, waiting for you. You didn't come, I thought Blade had you."

"Petey caught me but I got away." I find her in the dark and put the pizza box in her hands. "Here."

She takes a breath. "Where'd you get this?"

"Somebody gave me half a pizza. You eat it all. I already ate."

She chews and sighs, a soft sound in the dark.

I dig in my pocket. "Here's some money. Ten dollars. I know you gotta buy those vitamin pills so the baby grows good."

"I can't take your money, J."

"I can get more. He wants me to come back."

"Who?" Her voice is hard. "Come back for what?"

"The . . . artist I met. I met an artist. And he pays me pizza and ten dollars for sitting."

"What do you mean 'sitting'?"

"He pays me to sit and he makes a model of my head with clay and later he'll turn it into iron."

"You're crazy. You've always been a little loose, but now you're making things up."

"He's in the building on the other side of the fence. One of them rich people like we watched that time. He's an artist, name's Bill. He paid me ten dollars to sit on a stool and he made a statue of my head."

"You're messing with me."

"Nope. He bought the pizza, then gave me the money. Said he'd make a clay head of you, too, 'cept I told him you couldn't get through the basement window."

"I'd stick in the window like a cork in a bottle."

We both laugh at the picture, then grow quiet. She's thinking and I'm wondering about the head he was making of me.

"It's really something to see . . . ," I start.

"What?"

"The way he moves the clay around with his thumbs. Pretty soon I could see me inside it, waiting to come out."

"Sounds like you liked it."

"Watching him made me want to do it."

"So you're going back?"

I didn't say anything, but I knew I would.

To see if I could get another pizza.

To see if I could get ten more dollars for Layla.

More.

To see if I could move the clay like he did.

"You come sit next to me on the bench here." Her voice is low and I move to her, put my arms around her shoulders. She holds me around the waist and we sit like that in the dark.

I think she's just breathing but then I know she's crying.

"I'm scared."

"It'll be all right."

"I hate it here."

I hold her tighter. "It'll be all right."

Like I know.

Like I know anything.

Me and Layla spent the night in the basement with the lights off because she couldn't go home.

"Ma lost her night job," Layla tells me. "Got mean drunk when she came home. Blamed me for getting pregnant. Blamed me for everything."

"Like always," I say. We have that in common, getting blamed for everything that's wrong.

We slept some, talked some, cried some.

Just after the light comes through the little window, Layla goes back upstairs because she knows her ma left for her day job. But I go outside and through the alley and into the other building, back to my place. I wanna see about working with clay today.

I look out the window, but Bill isn't up yet. And even my Eskimo jacket can't stop the cold. Cold comes in like a snake, crawling around inside my clothes. My feet hurt for a long time, don't stop hurting until I can't feel them anymore.

Finally Bill wakes up. I watch him move back and forth. He goes past windows without looking until finally, when he's putting water in a teakettle, he looks up and sees me.

He opens the window. Steam comes off the sink and outside. He looks warm.

"Good morning, J. How long have you been there?"

"Just got here." No sense telling him everything. "Thought I'd see how you're doing."

"I'm fine. Since you're probably not going to school today . . ." He pauses and when I shake my head, he continues, "Come over and have some oatmeal and then we can work for a while. I didn't finish what I started last night."

"See you at the door." I go out to the middle of the building and start climbing out through the basement window.

Petey.

Another man is with him, name of Slipper, who's high all the time, worse than Petey.

They're by the Dumpster, but they don't see me so I pull my head back in. They're out early looking for something. I can see their breath in the freezing air and I know they're not out this early and in this cold unless Blade sent them for something.

For someone.

Only one thing Petey could be looking for 'cause there isn't any money to be made on the street this time of day.

He's looking for me.

Blade's got everything God made—money, connections uptown, the Big M car, the Glock Nine, women. Everyone on this street is either scared of him or working for him and it's not fair that he wants me, too.

But I know that when I got away from Petey, I made Blade look bad 'cause Petey works for Blade, and Blade doesn't like looking bad. Blade can't let that be.

I move across the basement to rooms I don't usually go in, wade through trash almost to my knees, to another window on the other side of the building.

Petey's so drunk he thinks he can stand by a Dumpster and catch me. His brains are nothing but mush from the drugs.

I climb outside, take the long way around the block to the other world, and I see Bill at the door. Waiting for me.

I slip inside. Warm. Safe. Good smells. He hands me a bowl of something tan covered with brown sugar, flecked with dark things.

"What are those?"

"Raisins. Don't you like them?"

"Sometimes." I shrug. "What are they?"

"Grapes. You dry grapes in the sun and they turn into raisins."

I eat the whole bowl and it's so hot and sweet it hurts my teeth, but good. I wish I could take some back for Layla. He puts the bowls in the sink when we're done and then slides the stand with my head out from a corner.

The head looks different from when I saw it last. Twisted or something, like I'm looking over my shoulder. There's nothing below the head, but the way the statue is looking, you know there's a shoulder down there. You can almost see the whole body below the head even though there's nothing but air and the post for the stand.

"Can you teach me to do that?"

He looks up quickly, surprised, smiles.

"I can help if you want to try sculpting."

He finds another small worktable, puts it in front of my stool and drops a lump of clay on it as big as both of my fists.

"What do I do?"

"Put your hands in the clay. Learn the texture and get used to the feeling."

"I want to do what you did. How do I make the clay look like what I can see in my head?"

"You have to work awhile before the clay shows you things that aren't there yet."

"But I . . . I want to make Layla."

He inhales sharply and studies my hands on top of the clay.

He comes over to the stand and looks into my eyes like he's seeing me for the first time. "Do you have a picture of her in your mind?"

"Sure. Layla's like the other side of me."

"Do you love her?"

"What's that got to do with making her come out of the clay?" I frown at him.

His face changes and he steps back quick, like he's said something he shouldn't have or done what he shouldn't. Like he's worried that he's made me mad.

"Working with the clay is . . . it's about a kind of love. You have to see things like you love them. Whether it's Layla or a brick . . . you have to see inside them to make the clay show you what's there."

How do you love a brick? But I can see he's happy talking like this, even if it is crazy. "How do I start?"

"Here." He takes my hands in his. I try to pull away but he holds firm, placing my hands gently on the lump of clay before he lets go. "Knead the clay, work your fingers into the clump. Learn how the clay moves under your hand. Feel how much pressure you need, and sense the difference against your fingertips and your knuckles and the heel of your hand. Start to try to make the shape round, like a head. Just work at that and, when you can see her, when you can see Layla's head in your hands, then I'll show you how to add clay and make the nose, lips, ears . . ."

So I start.

Warm, slow hands in the cool, soft clay, just trying to make it round.

I start.

10

Time stops. I don't know how to say it another way. I stop thinking of when, only thinking of what. No more whens or ifs.

Layla in the clay.

She's in there, waiting to come out. I use my fingers to try to find her. Like she's hiding and I've got to find her and bring her out.

I don't think of where I am when I'm working. Everything else goes away, this room, the neighborhood, the building on the other side of the block, Blade and Petey, I even forget Bill is there, listening, watching.

I don't know how long we've been working but when I look up he's looking at me. Not the way he was studying me when he sculpted me, but . . . I dunno, nice somehow. Nobody ever looked at me like that before.

"What?" I say.

"You were talking to yourself."

"I was?"

"Yeah. Who's Blade?"

"He's . . . over on my side of the block."

"He sounds like a very bad man."

"He's badder than words can say." I think about telling Bill about how Blade got his name, about the drugs and the money and the girls, and Petey hunting me for him, but Bill wouldn't believe me, wouldn't get it. "I don't even know words bad enough for Blade."

"Isn't there something you could do? Call the police?"

Now I *know* he's shining me on. "The police? Call the cops to come to my side of the block and do something with a drug dealer?" I laugh. Not a real laugh. Through my nose. "There's not enough police in the whole world to take the drug dealers out of my neighborhood. . . . 'Sides, I call them, they'll think I'm playing them. I'm just some dumb-ass kid on a phone. They won't come."

"What if I call them? Will they come then?"

"It won't matter anyway because Blade'll know before they get there. His people on the street tell him. The cops get there and there's nothing to see, nobody to arrest. Then they go away and Blade is still here. Only then he's pissed.

"You're over here warm and safe. We're stuck with Blade, who knows how to hurt people. . . . Don't call, it won't do any good anyway. There's only one way to stop Blade." We look at each other in the silence before I continue, "But even then, another Blade will just come along. . . . Nothing works out on our side of the block."

Bill looks down, toys with a piece of clay, stares out the window for a few seconds and then goes back to his work. I look at mine. I see something coming so I just let my fingers push here, pinch there, make a line with my fingernail. They're short 'cause I'm all the time chewing on them, but they make a line if I use the edge, and I see an eye, then another, a corner of lip.

"God."

I hear it in back of me and jump. Bill came up on me and I didn't even hear him.

"What?"

"Is that Layla?" He reaches out like he wants to touch her face but then he pulls his hand back. "It's . . . What is she afraid of?" His voice is hoarse.

He sees that. I didn't know it was even in the clay. But now I see it in the corners of her eyes. I know. I know what she's afraid of, but I lie—I shrug like I don't know.

He squints. "Her eyes off to the side like that, look-ing back almost like she sees . . ."

We don't say anything, but we both know that it's a monster she's looking at.

Blade.

11

Three days go by and I go to Bill's each day and we work together. He studies me while I work the clay. He doesn't do just one head, he does three, then four. All of me. But each one is different. In one I'm smiling because I was thinking of Layla having a baby. What the baby would be like. Cute, I know, 'cause it's from Layla, and it'll smile a lot. At Layla. And me.

Bill pays me ten dollars and gives me a pizza every day. I meet Layla every night and we sit in the dark and talk in whispers, sleep in the basement, stay away from her apartment and her ma, who still hasn't found another night job.

"Petey's looking for you," Layla says the third night in the basement. "He came to my place looking for you."

"Petey couldn't find himself if he was looking in a mirror."

"He's mad, his eyes were twitching when he said your name."

"Petey's all talk."

"I don't know. He scares me."

I want to say, You're scared all the time, Layla. But I don't. She's right to be scared and I should listen.

I should have listened.

At Bill's the next morning, I do two heads. Layla. Then Petey, but I don't know why. Bill said to make what I think about most in my head, and Petey's in there.

Every now and then Bill comes over to show me how to make my clay look better. He uses his thumb here or there and I can see what I was trying to do.

While we work he tells me about himself. He's twenty and, he says, should be in college. Where I live, no one even makes it through high school. His parents are upset that he dropped out. I think on that for a while. Folks on my side of the block don't get upset, hell, they don't even notice when you stop going to school. He says he didn't have enough time for art when he was going to classes and he's applied for something he calls a grant. Like a loan, I figure.

"It's enough to rent this place for a few years and buy the clay to work, get a few pieces cast in bronze from time to time. I'll sell what I can, buy materials. Keep going."

I might not know much about anything else he's talking about, but I know what it means to keep going.

I work on the heads while he talks. After three days it seems like we've been doing this forever. I wish we could keep doing this forever.

Bill says, "You're good, J."

And I say, "No, you're shining me on."

But he says, "No, you're really good. You have real talent. I mean, look at this Petey guy. He could pose for a statue of the devil. He just *looks* evil. And you caught it. I've never seen anybody without any training who could do anything like this. J, you really are amazing."

It's nice to have somebody tell you you're good at something. I don't think I ever heard anyone say anything like that to me before.

"I got to talk to Layla about this."

"Of course. Tell her I said you have real talent and it would be a shame to waste it."

Waste. I get a picture in my mind of a boy, a skinny boy with rat bites and bad teeth. I see that boy and how I could find him in the clay.

I know who the boy is.

And maybe written near the bottom of the statue, the word:

Waste.

Then I see another head and body. My mother before she went away, on the couch, stoned. I can see another head, Layla's ma, and then I see an old wino frozen on the grate, and five-dollar crack whores working the street.

And I know, I *know* that I can do them all and call them all *Waste*.

But that was before Petey got Layla.

Petey knows I have to come after her so he takes her and keeps her in his place on the ninth floor.

The way I find out is that I leave Bill's building and I'm heading back with pizza and money for her. When I get to the alley, in the dark, a boy name of Mohamud is standing by the Dumpster.

He's not seven years old and he works for Petey already. Skinny, near dead, always got snot dripping out his nose. He's like a rat hiding back in the dark by the Dumpster.

I see him before he sees me. I smell him. He's filthy. But I pay him no mind till he steps out.

"J—Petey says to come see him."

I stop. "Now, why would I want to do that?"

"He says if you don't come, he'll beat Layla so she's hurt on the inside."

"Layla . . ."

"He's got her up there. In his place on nine. He's keeping her until you come."

"You see her?"

"Yeah."

"He hurt her?"

"Not yet. But he will if you don't come. Said for me to tell you."

"You told me. You go on out of here."

I wait until he's gone and I go into the basement where the furnace room is dark. I hide the pizza even though I know the rats will find it. I hope something will be left when we get back.

I think that. I really think I'm going to go up there and get her. I believe that I'll get Layla and we'll eat pizza together in the dark again.

The best way is to just give myself to Petey, promise him anything to let me take Layla away. He won't kill me, he might beat me some, but I've been beat before. He'll keep me alive to work for Blade. I'll do anything, say anything, to get Layla right now.

My hands are shaking and my heart is pounding hard in my ears and my chest. I feel sweaty under my arms, but I'm cold and numb everywhere else.

I'll go straight up to Petey right now and he'll take me and let Layla go and that's it. That's the way this will play out.

This is the first time I go up the front of the building since I can remember. I walk like I own the stairs and head up to Petey's place. I'm out of breath when I get up there and I think about Bill's building, right next door, where the elevators work. No Petey, no Blade. You have trouble and you call the cops. They come.

Petey's door.

I stop.

If I'd known what was in that apartment, I wouldn't have knocked. If I'd known what was waiting I'd have walked backwards down the stairs and backed time up, a day, two days, four days, six days, to when Petey caught me and I got away. Before Bill. Before the clay. Then I'd let Petey take me, bust me up, give me to Blade. . . .

But I don't know what's in that apartment.

So I knock.

Petey opens the door. Smiles. "I knew you'd come."

"Let Layla go."

"Can't do it right now, boy. She nodded off." And he opens the door and I see her by the window in a chair. Head back funny. Mouth open.

"What did you do to her?"

Petey grabs me, drags me in the room and slams the door.

"She went crazy on me when I brought her up here. Ripped my face. So I had to quiet her down."

I see a cut down his cheek still bleeding. I jerk free and go over to Layla.

I touch her cheek. Cold. I lean over her face and listen, shake her. No breath.

Petey laughs, wasted out of his mind. "Guess I quieted that girl down too much."

Sometimes, I think, sometimes they bring them back. You see it on TV all the time. Call 911 and the ambulance drivers give them a shot and do something to their chest. . . .

No phone here.

Downstairs. Pay phone by the entry. Sometimes it works.

I hit Petey with a lamp from the table and when he bends over I hit him again in the side of his head. He stays down.

"I have to leave you, Layla. Gotta get the ambulance . . ."

But the phone is broke, and when I pound on doors and finally find somebody with a cell to call 911, I know, I know . . .

Too late. Too late.

I go back up there and sit by Layla, hold her hand. I don't feel anything except cold.

Petey starts to come around and I hit him again with

the lamp. Hit him so hard that he never comes around again.

Then I go back and sit with Layla again until, finally, they come and take her. A man says, "Another overdose," but I shake my head.

"No. Not Layla. Layla's . . . she's good. A good girl. She'd never . . ."

"What happened to the one on the floor?"

"He was keeping her here when she wanted to leave. I hit him."

"I'll have to call it in to the police."

I nod. Doesn't matter. Nothing matters.

They put Layla in a bag. Black bag with a zipper. I see them zip it up past her face. She's there, then she's gone.

Then I'm gone. I hear more sirens and I know it's the cops coming. Sure, they come now, called by the ambulance. Time for me to leave before the cops get here. Nothing I can tell them, anyway. Nothing to say to change anything. She's still gone.

'Cept in my head. She's there. I hear her laugh and I know that I will till I die, then some. Layla, I think, Layla.

Layla, I'm sorry.

13

Sometimes you move to the left, sometimes you move to the right, and sometimes you stay still and wait until the bad passes.

You stop moving too long, you're done.

I'm working for Blade now.

After they took Layla away in the black bag, I hid from the cops in the basement. I sat in the dark that whole night and then the next day. Rats ate the pizza I brought for Layla, ate the cardboard box, too, and I sat there missing her, thinking about her.

Thinking about Blade.

He's the reason.

He paid Petey.

He made Petey hurt Layla.

He had to pay.

Someday.

I'd make him pay.

Someday.

But I'd have to go slow to get close to him.

The word was out that I killed Petey, and Blade liked that: killing Petey made me tough, so he asked me to work for him. My first job: standing on the corner with a cell to warn him if the cops come.

Fine.

I got time. Could take a day, could take a week. He pays me a little money, I hustle some more, I buy a Glock Nine with a magazine that holds more bullets than God made.

Someday.

Someday I'll get close to Blade. Someday we'll be alone. Doesn't matter if it's a week, a month, a year. When we're finally alone, the very first second that we're alone, Blade's going to die.

Someday.

Meantime I work the street, make money, get good shoes, and every night I watch Bill.

I never go back to his apartment, never talk to him. But every night when I miss Layla and the hurt is bad, I go to my place in the basement and I sit in the dark and watch Bill across the fence.

Bill keeps making heads, some that look like me,

some from pictures. I sit in the dark every night and watch him.

It's like he knows I'm there. He'll turn and look out the window, look across the fence at the building I'm in, but I'm in the black night and he can't see me. He'll look sad, turn and go back to work, and I think . . . I think . . .

Someday, I'll go back.

Someday Blade will be gone and I will go and sit in the window until Bill sees me.

I'll say, "Hi, Bill."

And he'll smile and say, "Hi, J. Come over. I'll order a pizza."

Someday, I'll go back.

Someday I will make Layla come out of the clay and then Bill will show me how to make her into bronze so she lasts forever, so there will always be a Layla like I see her in my head.

Someday.

When Blade is gone.

Someday.

JO-JO
THE DOG-FACED
GIRL

THE TIME BEFORE

Before the dogs, Jo didn't have a family.

All her life, her parents—or, as she thought of them, the Biologicals—were drunk, blind drunk, mean drunk, fighting with each other and screaming at her every night.

Mostly, They didn't notice Jo. Which was good. Because when They saw her, She hit and He tried to touch. Jo learned to be invisible. And to push her dresser against the door of her room.

Before the dogs, she would move silently through the trailer to her room, where she would hide, alone in her special safe place—a shallow alcove in the trailer wall behind her bed, near the floor, where a propane bottle had once been stored.

In the mornings, she ate cold cereal, simple food that she could get for herself while they slept off the drunk. In the evenings, she ate leftovers from the fast-food containers they dropped on the kitchen counter on their way to the couch with a new bottle.

She wore hand-me-downs and garage-sale finds and out-of-season pieces from the sale racks at discount stores, always too big and either too soft and worn, or stiff and cheap-feeling.

Before the dogs, she didn't have friends. She saw how the other children at school looked at her—the sneers and the stares, the peeks at her out of the corners of their eyes before they glanced away quickly.

They must know, she thought, about how her life had made her ugly. The teachers looked at her with pity. She thought total strangers walking down the street could look at her and see the rips in the cloth of her life.

Before the dogs, she thought—no, she knew—that it would always be that way, and she had learned to shoulder it and taught herself to look past other people, glazing her eyes to not see what was in their faces.

She drifted through lonely days and lonesome nights and ripped, empty years.

But when Jo was twelve, it all changed.

2

The Biologicals were not her family. The people at school were not her friends.

Her true family was the dogs. Her only friends were the dogs.

Jo's first dog was a small terrier that a neighbor had left behind after the sheriff had showed up with papers in a file folder. There had been a lot of yelling at the front door. Jo watched the truck pull away, loaded with boxes and a few pieces of furniture, the dog forgotten, still tied to the fence.

Jo ran to him before the dust settled in the driveway, crouching on her haunches and slipping the chain clasp off his collar. She read the tag, MIKE, and whispered his name.

He rested his chin on her knee and sighed at the sound of her voice, and she felt something warm and new flutter inside her at the sound. She rose and he followed her back to her yard and into her room, both knowing that now they belonged to each other.

Mike curled up next to her every night when they went to sleep, his head nestled alongside her leg, exhaling in quiet thanks, just as he had that first day in the yard.

A few weeks later, a skinny brown mutt loped into the yard and sat next to her and Mike on the steps of the trailer. As if he'd always been there and wasn't about to leave.

Jo could tell he'd been a stray, living alone on the streets, because he was so skinny she could count his ribs, and the pads of his paws were ripped up and raw. Jo snuck into the living room, and while They yelled at each other, she rifled through Her purse and stole a twenty-dollar bill. She bought a pound of cheap hamburger to fatten this hungry dog up. And she went to the drugstore to buy ointment to rub on his sore paws. After They fell asleep, she lifted the new dog into the bathtub to wash away the dirt and grime with baby shampoo so his eyes wouldn't sting. She dried him carefully with her bath towel. Then she gently removed all the burrs and knots from his fur with her own comb and brushed his coat until it gleamed and he was perfect and beautiful.

Jo named him Carter because a nice man named Carter had worked behind the bar at the tavern where the Biologicals used to take her when she was little. She'd tried to sleep in the back booth while They drank. She remembered that Carter had always smiled at her, even though it had been years since They'd bothered to take her anywhere with Them.

Carter the dog smiled too. And he'd bring the Frisbee back to her exactly five times. Not four. Never six. Always five. Carter didn't care if the Frisbee was thrown fast five times in a row—*zip, zip, zip, zip, zip*—or if the game was dragged out, maybe one throw every half hour. After the fifth throw, no matter how long it took, Carter would lie on the ground, the Frisbee between his paws, and pant—or chuckle, *heh heh heh*—and the game was done for the day.

Then, a few days after Carter came home, Jo saw a small Border collie in a box outside the grocery store with a sign that said FREE PUPPIES.

Jo named her Betty after a grandmother she'd read about in a book. The grandmother had baked and sewed and read aloud from the Bible at night.

Although Betty was the youngest, and the only female, she was the protector of the group, her eyes constantly scanning their surroundings. Her ears would flatten back against her head, the hair on her neck would rise and a low growl would rumble deep in her throat if she saw anything she didn't like—squirrels, the

Biologicals, the rattling old pickup that didn't have a muffler and came roaring into the trailer park each night.

Jo's family: Mike, Carter and Betty.

If the Biologicals noticed the dogs, They didn't say anything. And the dogs learned quickly to ignore Them, looking away and padding silently through the trailer behind Jo, but keeping themselves always between Jo and Them.

And now, instead of dreading the night because it was lonely and long, Jo loved it because they slept together, the four of them. And in the dark, she could not tell where one ended and another began—dog heat, dog breath, dog dreams—so close they were like one.

Even the screaming and fighting were muffled, distant, less somehow than when she'd been alone. All she heard was the sighs and the yawns and the soft *uff uff uff* of the dogs' breathing in the night. With the dresser pushed against the door, Jo and her dogfamily were safe.

Once, late, Jo had awakened to see the dogs bathed in the soft moonlight that came through the window. She moved to the foot of the bed with them and sat in the silver light, felt it glow on the skin of her cheek and move into her to the rhythm of the dogs' breathing. She closed her eyes and, timing her breath to match theirs, she inhaled the moonlight. She smelled the silver-nickel of the moonlight on the sides of her tongue and through her nose and in the back of her mouth *with* the dogs, *of* the dogs, *as* the dogs.

Four doghearts breathing together in the quiet, bright dogmoon dognight.

Before Mike and Carter and Betty, Jo had had bad dreams about the terror that came when she couldn't run, when she couldn't get to her bedroom with the dresser pushed against the door fast enough. For years she'd had the same dream, or, really, the same memory in the night. But once the dogs were with her, the memories stopped. For a few nights, she'd jerked awake, panting and sweaty, heart pounding, stomach in knots, a scream choking her, but then she'd see Mike and Carter and Betty watching, guarding, their eyes soft.

Now the dreams were good. When she closed her eyes in half-sleep with her hands wrapped in their fur and felt their legs pedal as they slept, she knew she could run with them, *be* them in her dreams. They'd run through grass that tickled their bellies and her feet, run through green dappled woods with the speckled light shining on their coats and her hair. Never tiring, never stopping, free and smooth and fast and light, almost flying.

Four doghearts together.

Jo and her dogs were safe in the night, but she couldn't leave them alone with the Biologicals during the day when she went to school.

The back edge of the trailer park bordered a gully filled with thick brush that led to a small woods. Once, when Mike had been chasing rabbits, he'd led them to an old fort that had been abandoned by neighborhood kids, a rickety lean-to made of wooden pallets with a piece of plywood for a roof and a door with twine hinges that could be propped shut.

Jo brought the dogs here on her way to school each morning. She'd taken an old sleeping bag from an empty trailer and wrapped it in a large plastic garbage bag to keep it dry. Every morning she shook it out and made a nest for her family next to a clean bucket of fresh water. She fed them bread and peanut butter, sometimes a few cans of sardines, dry dog food when she could slip fives and tens from His wallet or Her purse.

During school, she imagined her dogfamily, curled up asleep, waiting for her, hidden safely in the woods. She wouldn't look at the people around her, but past them, seeing Mike and Carter and Betty instead.

Always the dogs.

Only the dogs.

3

Jo could have lived that way forever, with the rest of the world at a distance. Especially after He left.

After a particularly horrible fight, when the neighbors started yelling to "shut the hell up," He took his things and left.

Good. There would be no more touching. Ever.

That made Her easier to live with too. She never tried to hit anymore and she was gone most of the time or passed out in her room.

Jo developed a routine. Every day she got up early. The dogs would be sitting next to her, shifting impatiently to nudge her awake. She'd slip out of bed and pick up the clothes that she'd dropped on the floor the night before. She'd dress quickly and the dogs would follow her through the trailer and out to do their business in the yard. Jo would clean up after them with old newspapers and then take them for their morning walk.

Back at the trailer, Jo would eat cold cereal and milk and fry one egg until it was hard, for a sandwich to take for lunch. Then she'd take the dogs to their hideaway in the woods, feed them, and head out.

Four blocks north and then two blocks east to the middle school. Once she was clear of the trailer park and past the first corner, the streets were tree-lined, with pretty houses, small but neat and with big yards. She didn't look in the windows as she walked by or even glance at the yards because maybe everything in those homes was perfect, like on TV, and she tried not to look at things that made her feel even more ugly and broken.

She moved silently through the day, talking to no one, being talked to by no one, head down, eyes fixed on the floor. She went to school and learned to read and write and remember the *i*-before-*e*-except-after-*c* rule and how to change fractions into percentages and figure out when trains coming from different directions at different speeds would meet. She completed all her homework and took the tests and paid attention in class, although she never raised her hand. When called upon by her teachers, she answered so softly she could hardly be heard.

She never ate in the cafeteria. Too many people, too

close together. She went to the playground and sat on the side of the building where the wind didn't blow and the sun felt warm on her skin. She ate her sandwich and thought of the doghearts waiting for her.

She rolled in the love like a dog rolling in the grass.

She thought about how Carter would narrow his eyes when he was listening; how Mike would drag his rear left leg when he was tired; how Betty would sit straight and attentive if she was nervous. Jo remembered the differences between their different tail wags—fast and side to side when she came to get them after school or in frantic circles when they played catch. And she examined the growls and barks and howls and yips and whines they made as if she were studying a foreign language.

She imagined the warmth of them tucked next to her in sleep, saw the sun glinting in their eyes as they ran in the park, smelled that ripe-fresh-earthy-sweet-doggy smell when she'd bury her face in their fur.

Before, when she was very young, when she still noticed other people, kids at school had teased her because she never had playdates and wasn't enrolled in after-school activities and had weird clothes and didn't eat out of fancy lunch boxes or drink store-bought juice in foil packets with built-in straws. But she'd been with most of the same kids year after year, and once she'd stopped responding—looking right through them as if they weren't there—they stopped teasing. She knew they still stared, but they hid it better now that everyone was older.

One boy, though, Loren Haugen, kept taunting her. Her silence and indifference seemed to infuriate him and, unlike everyone else, he didn't know enough to ignore her.

A few weeks earlier, when he saw her sketching the dogs in her notebook before homeroom began, he'd hooted and called her the Dog Girl. Then he'd gotten his hands on an old book about early circuses, with pictures about the sideshows: Alligator Man, the human with alligator skin; the Bearded Lady, a homely woman with long facial hair; the Marvelous Tattooed Man, every inch of him tattooed; and Jo-Jo the Dog-Faced Boy, the Original Freak of Nature.

He'd thought that was hysterical, showed everyone the picture while pointing at Jo, and he shouted that name after her in the hallway.

Jo looked at Loren's leering face, but his sneer blurred in her sight and instead she saw Mike put his head on his paws and follow her with his eyes when she moved around their room, and Betty drop her chest to the ground and stick her rump in the air as she waited for Jo to slip the leash onto her collar, and Carter nuzzle Mike's ear and Betty's neck as they curled up in the

78

shack every morning to wait for Jo to come back from school.

She smiled: Jo-Jo the Dog-Faced Girl.

No, she thought, Jo the dogheart girl.

Even if they weren't with her, Jo's dogs still protected her from everything that hurt.

NOW

Weekends, Jo took Carter, Betty and Mike into the woods to run off the leash. She liked the privacy and quiet safety she felt among the trees. The dogs had taught her to see, to look for color and shape and movement. Out in the world, she looked away from people and kept her eyes down, but in the woods she could inspect everything around her.

At first everything was just green. The woods blurred together like the faces in school did.

But then she noticed how the dogs trotted along overgrown paths she hadn't discovered on her own. She studied how they brushed against low-hanging branches of leafy bushes thick with shiny red berries. She scrambled to keep up as they leapt over piles of dead leaves and fallen logs in single file, waiting for her on the other side.

The green wall of the woods changed after she copied the way the dogs peered at the trees. She saw leaves the color of moss and emerald and khaki and lime and olive, brown and beige and tan and gray and silver, all glowing under the yellow- and gold- and lemon- and honey- and wheat-colored sunshine that cut through the high branches in shafts.

Mike and Carter and Betty showed Jo all the shades of color in the whole wide world on display in the small woods behind the trailer park.

They'd run off barking, dashing through the trees and splashing into the small creek nearby, before coming back to sit by Jo and share her sandwich and talk.

After a lifetime of silence, she found that she had much to say. She told them everything.

But they never talked about the Biologicals or school: Jo had nothing to say about them and she didn't want Mike and Carter and Betty to know about ugliness.

Instead she told them about the books she read and the music she listened to on CDs at the library. They listened, watching her face, tails slowly wagging, ears twitching at the sound of her voice.

And they talked to her with their eyes and their bodies and their voices. With a limp and a soft groan, Mike told her about the aches he felt in his hip when it was damp. Carter showed her how funny it was to put a feral cat up a tree, dancing around the trunk and barking at the hissing cat high in the branches. Betty taught Jo how important it was to always stay close together; she would circle Jo and the boys, herding them in a tight cluster as they walked.

"You talk to your dogs?"

The voice came from behind. Jo wheeled around, startled. Betty, who had wandered away without Jo's noticing, was leading a girl toward her.

The girl was about Jo's age, though she was short and scrawny. She had dark eyes that pointed down at the outside corners, which made her look sad. Her eyelids were a little dark too, which made her seem even sadder.

Except that she was smiling. "Do they answer?"

"Always." Jo was surprised that she spoke to this strange girl instead of looking down and away. Immediately, she regretted talking about her dogworld.

Betty led the girl closer and they sat down next to Mike and Carter, who wiggled in happiness at this stranger's company. Betty shifted her weight, pressing her side against the girl's leg.

They all faced Jo, who sat, silent. This girl was so close. Jo had felt so safe in the woods, so alone and protected, that she hadn't kept her usual eye out for anyone nearby.

"See," the girl finally said, "this is where we have a

conversation. I say something like 'Those are beautiful dogs,' and you say, 'Thanks,' and then I say, 'What are their names?' and you . . ." She smiled and put a hand out, palm up, prompting Jo.

"Mike, Carter and Betty."

Betty leaned over and picked up the small branch that she had been carrying all morning because she was proud of the way it hung from her mouth. She placed it on the girl's lap.

The girl laughed. "Thank you! What a nice present— Er," and she turned to Jo, "I don't know which name is his."

"Her."

"Pardon?"

"She's not a boy dog."

"So it's Betty, then. I'm Rose."

"I'm Jo." She couldn't remember the last time she'd introduced herself to anyone. Had she *ever* done that?

All three of the dogs were looking at Rose with gentle curiosity, and Jo could tell that the boys enjoyed being petted by her. Jo liked the way Rose traced the stick with her fingers, following each crook carefully, before setting it back down on Betty's paws.

"So you and your dogs come to the woods to talk?" Rose asked, smiling.

"Uh-huh. Why are you here?"

"My yard backs to the trees." Rose pointed toward the neat houses on the pretty streets. "Sometimes I just go wandering. It's nice"—she looked away, blinking hard for a second—"to be outside. And I like how quiet it feels in the trees, you know?"

Jo nodded.

"I don't have dogs. My mother doesn't like dogs. No"—Rose paused and frowned, thinking—"it's not that she doesn't *like* dogs, it's just that she doesn't *know* about them. Does that make sense?"

"It does to me."

"She thinks they're a lot of work and mess up the carpet and carry bugs."

"That's not what they're about."

"I bet it would be wonderful to have—no, to be with dogs."

"It is."

"But we move too much too; my dad is a reorganization and downsizing consultant and so we're always going where his jobs are. I haven't even started school here yet. Not that— Well. What does your dad do?"

My dad drinks, my dad fights, my dad tries to touch, my dad left, Jo thought. She took three, four, five breaths before answering, "No dad."

"Oh. A mom?"

"Just the dogs."

Rose shot her a glance but sat quietly watching Betty snuffling Jo's ear.

"I didn't think I'd make any friends until I started school," Rose said, "but here you are in the woods."

"You don't want to be my friend."

"Why not?"

"Because I'm not the kind of"—Jo almost said "dog"—"person anyone wants to be friends with."

Jo stood and started to walk away. But the dogs stopped as Rose spoke:

"Neither am I."

5

One place Jo felt safe was the library.

Everything about the library was good.

It was warm in the winter and cool in the summer and always dry and safe and Jo never felt the stares at the library. The Biologicals had never been there, might not have even known it existed, for all Jo knew.

She would go to check out books on Saturday afternoon and Wednesday evening. There was an overgrown lilac bush near the reading room windows and Mike and Carter and Betty would crawl under the lowest branches and wait. She kept glancing out the windows, checking that she could always see the dogs hidden under the bush.

Jo loved books. Not as much as her dogs, and in a

different way, but pretty close. Every Saturday and Wednesday she'd pick out three books—novels, graphic novels, picture books, poetry, history, short stories, plays, mysteries, travel guides, equipment repair manuals, stories of aliens or myths or true crime. It didn't matter what she read.

What did matter was that when she read, she could forget how ugly her life was.

She read aloud to the dogs when they were in the woods or in her room with the dresser pushed across the door. They usually fell asleep, but even if they didn't pay attention, reading to them made the words go inside her the way the moonlight had gone into her, so that she felt-heard-smelled the words.

The day before, when Rose had been talking, Jo had seen the color of her words. She'd felt the hope in her voice. She'd tasted the loneliness in Rose's sentences. She understood that Rose had been trying to tell her something, with the words she used and the ones she didn't.

Still thinking about Rose, Jo checked out her books, gathered the dogs and headed home the short way, through the woods. She wasn't surprised to see Rose sitting on a stump near the edge of the trees.

Waiting for them.

Mike barked a happy greeting, Carter bounded over and Betty tried to make Jo hurry.

"I hoped you'd all be here today," Rose said.

"Betty's eyes tip up. Yours tip down."

"They do? I didn't know that."

"The dogs taught me to notice things."

"That's amazing."

"Dogs are better—" Jo stopped.

"Go on. What were you going to say? Better than . . . ?"

"Better than people." Rose nodded and Jo went on. "Humans aren't as smart as dogs. Even though they think they are. Even people who like dogs and have them as pets don't always understand how smart dogs are and how much they know."

"What do they know?"

"How to see, smell, run. They can do all those things better than humans." Jo took a breath. "They feel more too. Dogs know how to love better than people."

Both girls watched Mike settle his chin on one of Rose's feet and close his eyes. Carter, lifting his front paws, rested them on Rose's lap and stared into her face, and Betty rolled onto her back, presenting her tummy for Jo to scratch. Jo peeked up from Betty and saw Rose smiling at her.

"I bet they're good listeners, too," Rose said. "I like the way they watch you when you talk, and look back and forth between us when we speak."

"Dogs hear things we can't. Sometimes I believe they can hear me think."

"Do you really think so?" Rose sounded worried. "Can they do that with everyone?"

"I'm sure they can."

"Oh." Rose stared at her shoe, pushed a small rock back and forth with her foot. A sharp beep from her wristwatch startled everyone. The dogs jumped up. "I have to get home now." Rose headed into the bushes toward her house. "I'll see you another time."

She stopped, ran back and kissed each dog on the nose before smiling at Jo and turning to leave.

Jo watched the dogs watching Rose disappear, their eyes pinched and worried, all three of them panting and uneasy as the sound of her moving through the under-brush faded away.

Really bad things froze time, Jo knew, or worse—time even seemed to go backwards, so that you would live and relive painful moments over and over. . . .

But time went fast when she was talking with Rose.

So, bad things made time go slowly and good things made time go fast.

"Rose is a good thing," she told the dogs, who were still staring into the woods after Rose. "But you already know that."

6

As if they'd agreed to, Jo and Rose met in the woods late the next morning, a sunny Sunday, greeting each other with shy smiles. They walked silently through the trees, listening to the crunch of leaves beneath their feet and catching glimpses of the dogs in the brush as they chased each other before circling back to the girls. The quiet was full and warm and Jo felt a rightness in the day and in the way her steps matched Rose's.

"I brought a picnic lunch." Rose poked her backpack. "Well, my mother packed it. There's enough for us all."

"Here." Jo pulled a plastic bag out of her backpack and thrust it into Rose's hands. "I brought something too."

Earlier that morning, as Jo was taking the dogs out, she'd seen Her drop a wad of cash outside the car as She lurched home. Jo had pocketed the cash and headed to the pet store to get some canned dog food, a special treat. While she was there, she had seen something she knew would be perfect for Rose.

Rose reached into the bag and pulled out a baseball cap with a picture of a Border collie that looked like Betty. The cap said DOGS RULE. She looked up at Jo and beamed.

"Put it on."

Rose slipped the cap on. It came down over her ears, so Jo gently removed it, adjusted the strap, and set it back. "Perfect."

"Yeah, it is. You know that? It's absolutely perfect."

"Dogs always are."

"It's the best present I've ever gotten," Rose said.

It was the only gift Jo had ever given anyone.

They sat, turning their faces up to the sun and breathing in the yellow warmth together.

"Is it hard to understand your dogs?" Rose asked.

"If you don't know each one well, it probably is."

"Can you help me know them like you do?" Rose took off her cap and studied the picture of the Border collie.

"I think so."

"What do I do?"

"You have to learn how to see them."

91

Rose laughed. "That's not hard; they're right in front of me."

"No. Really see them, how they are."

"What do you mean?"

"Close your eyes."

"Why?"

"Close your eyes to see better." Rose smiled, and so did Jo. "Close them tight."

Rose closed her eyes and Jo noticed again how dark and smudgy Rose's eyelids were compared to the paleness of her cheeks. Jo wanted to reach out and touch her. She raised a hand, but pulled back. Mike, who had been watching, put his paw on Rose's leg.

"Now tell me how the dogs look, what you see when you think of them."

"One is black-and-white and one is brown and one is almost all white. . . ."

"More."

"Um . . . Mike is the small mutt, Carter is the brown one, and Betty is the black-and-white Border collie."

"And?"

"Betty has one ear that sticks up and the other flops down, but wait, no, it's more like it goes straight out. The little guy, Mike, has a lower jaw that kind of juts out so that he looks like he might bite. And Carter, the brown one, has a triangular-shaped head with a flat top. Oh! And Betty has a bump that sticks up in the middle of her head. And Carter has gray hairs around his muzzle like a beard, and Mike's toenails are different colors, some are brown and some are white . . ."

She went on as memory fed on memory and the speckled light shone down through the tree branches, bathing Rose's face in soft green from the leaves.

Jo said, "Open your eyes. Touch the tops of their noses now. Run your hand back toward their eyes. When you do that they know you love them and want to know them. Now tell me how their fur feels, how each dog feels different from the other."

"Their ears are softer than the rest of their fur," Rose said. "Their noses are cold and wet and I think it tickles them when I touch their whiskers. My fingers go *bump-bump* along their ribs and I can feel how the sides of their chests dip into the tucks of their flanks just in front of their legs. They all have four toenails on their back feet, and four together but one higher up on their front paws."

Rose pictured more details about the dogs as her hands roamed their fur. "Mike lowers his right shoulder and whines when he wants your attention. Carter has short or long tail wags, depending on whether or not he can see you. Betty is the loudest; she has rumbly growls and quick barks and grunty sighs and low howls, depending on what she's trying to tell you."

Rose talked until the sun started down, and Jo sat

with her eyes closed, seeing what Rose was imagining. They breathed together, the girls and the dogs. Jo wondered if all of their hearts were beating in time too.

When at last Rose stopped talking and opened her eyes, the dogs were lying between the girls, their backs against Jo, touching her legs but looking at Rose, listening.

Hearing her.

Knowing her.

Loving her.

"**I** have leukemia."

Rose's words turned everything dark. They were walking near the edge of the woods toward Rose's house in the late afternoon after she'd seen the dogs with her memory.

"I didn't know how to tell you. I'm sorry it came out so sudden." Rose talked very fast. "It's hard to say. For the longest time I thought if I didn't say anything, it would just go away."

No, Jo thought. What she just said, that ugly word, doesn't exist, isn't true.

"I'm going to have to go in again, soon, for more treatments. I just wanted you to know."

Jo matched the words in her mind to the pace of

their footsteps, slow and halting. No . . . she's a friend . . . to the dogs . . . and so my friend too. My first friend . . . my only friend . . . she can't . . . no . . . this was a good day . . . the best day . . . my only right and perfect day ever, and now . . .

She remembered then how carefully Mike and Carter and Betty studied Rose and how she had seen but not seen Rose's dry lips and bony hands and pale skin and skinny shoulder blades poking through her sweatshirt, and the dark smudges underneath her eyes. She remembered how gently they leaned when they rested against Rose and how sad their eyes were when they watched her.

"I already knew," she said.

"You did?"

"My dogs knew the first day. They've been trying to tell me. I didn't understand, though. I didn't want to."

Rose stopped walking. "How could they know?"

"They understand things people can't, because they see you. And they saw something they didn't like."

"I'm going to be fine, though." Rose lifted her chin and made her voice hard. "That's what everyone says. There's nothing to worry about, and in a few months this will all be behind me, and I just have to keep my spirits up until then."

Carter looked back at Rose. Mike sighed and sat on the path. Betty sneezed and shook her head once, hard.

Jo could tell that Rose was lying, just like the dogs

could. The only thing she didn't know was whether Rose knew she wasn't telling the truth.

There was nothing to say and so Jo was quiet as they stood together in the twilight. Once again, Jo wanted to touch Rose, the way she touched Mike when he trembled during a thunderstorm. But she'd never reached out to any person before. It took her three tries, lifting her hand and pulling it back, before she finally slipped her hand into Rose's.

Rose squeezed back. And held on tight.

8

Rose didn't come to the woods the next day. Or the next or the next or the next. Jo stopped counting the nexts, but the dogs lifted their noses to the sky, trying to catch Rose's scent, every time they went into the woods.

Jo moved through those endless days the way she had lived before the dogs came, frozen, stiff and hollow. The dogs snapped at each other with sharp growls and quickly bared teeth. They didn't run ahead of her the way they usually did as they moved through the trees, but they walked on either side and just in front, almost touching her.

Jo wondered if she'd imagined Rose. Had she made up someone to talk to, conjured someone who tried to see the dogs the same way she did? Invented a friend?

But then she saw Mike nosing around the stump where Rose had sat that second day. Carter dug at the spot where they'd all sat together the first day. Betty kept running back to the place where they'd eaten sandwiches together. And Jo knew.

Rose had been real.

Jo walked slowly, *Rose, Rose, Rose* thumping through her mind with each step. The dogs quickened their pace, though, and she had to trot to keep up with them.

They led her deep into the woods and then stopped next to the small stream. They sat in a line and watched the slow current tumble and roll the shallow waters. Jo didn't sit next to them as she normally would, but instead paced along the water's edge.

Rose. Rose. Rose.

No. No. No.

She felt like hitting something, like breaking something. She shuddered, thinking how like the Biologicals that idea was. She looked to the dogs. For once they weren't watching her every move. All three dogs had their eyes fixed on the flat, broad rock that loomed above the waterline in the center of the creek, listening to the water splash on the sides.

The boulder was beautiful—gray speckles and green flecks and streaks of icy white quartz. The rock glistened where the water hit the sides and made it wet.

Jo thought it might be magic, something she could touch and wish upon, like in a fairy story. She waded into the stream, stood in the water up to her knees and laid her hand flat against the rock. Rose. Rose. Rose.

She dropped her chin onto her chest, staring down at the water trickling past her legs. Through the burning in her eyes, she saw the sudden appearance of brown and white and black.

The dogs had paddled out and were scrambling up, their front claws scratching and their back legs pedaling to clamber up to the flat top. They sat, each facing in a different direction, and watched the creek flow past their rock island. Jo climbed up and looked down too.

The water had to run around the boulder to keep flowing. It couldn't move the stone but had to curve and ripple around the edges.

The stream, she thought, was like everything ugly in her whole life, everything broken and damaged in the entire world. But the rock was like what the dogs had given her, what Rose had given her.

And nothing could ever take that away. She had a family now, and a friend, and no matter what happened, that would never change.

WHAT COMES AFTER

Jo had been sitting on the rock with the dogs for most of the afternoon when Betty jumped up as if she'd been stung by a bee, leaping into the water. Mike and Carter yipped at Jo until she followed, sliding off the rock and wading to the bank. The dogs shook the water from their coats and then led Jo through the woods. She hardly dared hope they were right, but she saw that they were taking her to the other side of the woods, to the edge of Rose's yard. She held her breath and kept her eyes on the ground until they reached the yard.

Jo lifted her head. Rose was sitting in a lawn chair,

gazing at the woods, waiting for them. Her face lit up when they bounded out of the shade toward her.

She had a bandana tied awkwardly around her head. Jo could see that she was trying to hide her baldness. Rose wore a huge sweatshirt and was wrapped in a blanket. She had shearling moccasins on her feet.

"I didn't have a chance to tell you. . . ."

"I wanted to come and . . ." Jo couldn't finish her sentence.

"No one is very happy with me being outside." Rose gestured over her shoulder to the house. Jo saw a curtain flick in the window as someone peeked out. "But I said I wanted to sit in the sunshine for a while."

"That's always a good idea."

"I . . . I need to know some things that I think the dogs understand. No one else can tell me, and they . . . well, I think they— Oh, I don't know how to say it right."

"I understand what you mean."

"My parents don't know what I think about," Rose said. "They tell me there's hope, that the doctors say I'll go into remission after this treatment. And they want it so bad that I . . ."

Jo didn't respond, but Mike placed his paw on Rose's arm the way he always thanked Jo after she fed him.

"Do your dogs always know what's going to happen before it does?"

"Probably. The sky's blue right now, but it's going to

rain later. They step fast and light, like they're doing right now, when rain is about to come."

"Because they see what we can't and so they know what we don't?" Rose's eyes looked tired.

"Yes, I think that's it."

Rose's voice was soft. "Do they know what happens when somebody dies?"

"Yes. They must know that."

"Oh, I'm so glad. I've been so—" Rose inhaled, quick and sharp.

When Rose broke off, Betty turned to gaze at her. Betty pushed her forehead up into Rose's hand and slowly wagged her tail.

Rose looked up at Jo for a second, a minute, a week, a year, all of time, as if they knew something together, just the two of them.

Jo took a huge breath and felt that same warm flutter she had when Mike had first laid his head on her thigh.

"The dogs make me feel safe," Rose said.

"Me too."

Rose smoothed the fur near Betty's crooked ear, carefully stroking it into a straight line, looking into Betty's kind brown eyes, which never left her face. Mike and Carter were pushing into her legs with their shoulders.

"They're more than just dogs, aren't they?"

Jo nodded. "They never hurt anyone and they know everything there is about love and all they want is to help us not be alone and scared. They never give up."

Rose said, "Could they help me?"

"Of course."

For the first time in years, Jo was crying. For the first time ever, she was crying for someone else.

Rose rested her hand in Jo's. They stayed still for a long time, their hands clasped as darkness fell, looking above the trees, where small white clouds were being gently pushed past the full moon by a soft wind.

Finally, the dogs stood with a jingling of collar tags, filling the air with the sound of bells.

ERIK'S RULES

1

"Jamie. Time to wake up."

I open my eyes and see Erik, my older brother, crouched next to where I'm sleeping on the floor. He's shaking me awake. The apartment is dark and he's whispering. "We've got to get moving. C'mon. Time to go."

I sit up, stretch and yawn while Erik rolls up his sleeping bag. He gestures to me and I slide out of my bag, slip my shoes on and tie the laces while he ties up my sleeping bag. We sleep in our clothes, so after rolling up our bedding and grabbing our backpacks and the duffel bag with our spare clothes, we're out the door.

He gives me a dollar when we get to his car before he goes to work.

I have $1.78.

That means I can afford a bagel for breakfast because, with tax, a plain bagel costs $1.21. If I'm smart, I'll only eat half and save the other half for lunch. I'm not that smart, though, so I'll eat the whole bagel this morning on the way to school and then my gut will be complaining this afternoon.

But I can usually fool my stomach by drinking enough water at the fountain to feel full. I'm into quick fixes. Quick fixes are the only thing I've got these days.

I don't have to worry about supper; Erik always brings me food. He works at the Burger Barn and his manager lets him have the patties that have been sitting in the warming tray long enough that they start getting dried up around the edges. No ketchup or mustard or pickles or onions or tomatoes or cheese, and by the time I get them, they're cold and rubbery and the buns are stale. But there's usually enough to eat to make me feel stuffed.

Erik and I ran away from home two years ago when I was ten and he was fifteen.

No. That's not quite right.

We drove away in the car he stole.

And what we left was no kind of home.

Erik's Rule #1: Don't talk about—don't even think about—what happened before.

"That's over," he said as we pulled away in the blue Toyota that belonged to some guy who was passed out in our mother's room.

I nodded.

"We're never going back there."

I nodded again.

"No one will ever try to hurt you again."

My brother doesn't talk much, and when he does, it sounds like rules, or warnings, or instructions. Not regular conversation. But that's okay because he never yells and all the words he uses are PG-13. Which is a nice change of pace.

Erik and I have been on the move ever since we left. I tried to remember exactly when that was, but I'm not good with dates so I can only guess. I know it was summertime, because for the first few weeks we camped out, kind of, spreading our sleeping bags in the storage shed at the beach and showering in the locker room.

We've slept in the office at the garage where Erik works part-time. Once, when Erik was dating a girl whose mom owned a dance school, we slept in the studio. That was the best deal yet—we crashed on the couches in the waiting room and soft music played all night long. But then the girlfriend, I can't even remember her name, started dating someone new, a guy whose little brother didn't want to sleep in her mom's lobby, probably, and we had to move on.

A few times we had nowhere else to go so we slept in Erik's car, the one we took when we left, just grabbed the keys off the floor near the pile of clothes and empty bottles like they belonged to us and didn't slow down, never looked back. Sleeping in the car was the worst. Toyotas might get good gas mileage and run really well, but they don't have much room.

Trying to sleep in the car was even worse than sleeping in the booths at the Burger Barn, which we did for a couple of weeks last winter. We were warm and dry, sure, but we reeked of old French fries and cleaning solution.

We've been staying with Trudy for about a month now. That means dropping our stuff in a corner of her living room and sleeping on her floor. Tru's the exgirlfriend of the garage manager where Erik works and I think she's just letting us stay with her to make Carl mad. I know we won't be here long.

Erik's Rule #2: We keep clean, we keep quiet, we keep moving.

Erik is trying to scrape together enough money for an apartment, but you've got to have three months' worth of rent—first, last and deposit—to get a place. We never manage to save enough.

It's not that he doesn't work hard, because he flips burgers during the lunch shift after he's spent the morning doing oil changes at Dwight's garage and before his job as the after-school custodian at a Catholic grade school. Everyone pays him cash, under the table, they call it, which means no checks or paperwork.

Erik keeps track of our money in a little notebook— he writes down what he makes and what we spend and what he saves in the zippered pouch on a cord around his neck under his shirt. I hate that little notebook because Erik always looks worried when he studies it.

We shop at the Goodwill for clothes and only go to the Laundromat every couple of weeks. But the Toyota needs gas so Erik can to get to work and he makes us take vitamins every day because he says the last thing we need is to get sick. The fake ID he bought from a guy who hangs out at the garage cost a ton, but he needs it in case he ever gets stopped on a traffic violation. And then there's all the money Erik needed to pay this shady guy Digger he met at the garage. Digger painted the car we stole and did something with the paperwork that made it look like it was legally ours so no one would know it was hot.

Erik gives me a buck or two every day for breakfast or lunch; I know he hates that it's either/or, but he doesn't eat both meals either. He says he's never really hungry until after he puts in a good day's work, but I can hear his stomach growling.

Erik and I might not have a place to live, but we have an address, because you've got to have an address to go to school. I don't know why, though, because all of the forms and permission slips and report cards come by email, which we check at the public library on the account that Grandpa set up years ago. We use Grandpa's old folks' home's address as ours and that keeps me legit at school. No one checks.

2

The worst part about being broke and not having a regular place to live is that I've always wanted a dog. But dogs—even more than people because you can't explain the situation to a dog and expect him to understand—need a warm place to sleep and good food every day. If I could do that for a dog, it would mean I'd have a home and three squares too. So I think wanting a dog is a better dream than hoping for a college education. For a guy like me.

Erik has always been great about finding cheap fun. Cheap is good, but free is better, so we've always liked to visit the dog run in the park.

We watch all the dogs and pick out which one we'd want to be ours. Erik likes the little ones that are feisty and don't know they're small enough to be eaten whole by the bigger dogs. I like the big ones that look like, if you could hear their thoughts, they'd be thinking, *Dunh dunhdunh,* in a really happy, punchy little hum.

Even when Erik's at work, I still like to go to the dog park. When I'm alone, I take my sketchbook.

I've been drawing, or trying to draw, ever since I saw a book at the library about paintings in caves in France. They were the first art ever, about hunting and hurting and dying. And the way I could see the people's lives in the paintings made me want to do the same thing.

Erik has never once hit me, but he said he would beat me raw if he ever caught me stealing.

Erik's Rule #3: It's nothing but trouble to want what you don't already have.

I think he meant: Don't take money or food or clothes. I'm pretty sure he doesn't consider it stealing when I take sketchbooks and the soft smudgy pencils from Mrs. Fitzgerald's art room at school.

Because he knows I have to draw or I'll lose it. When I'm hungry, cold, dirty or sick to death of wondering where we're going to sleep tonight, I can pull out one of my sketchbooks. A little while later, I'm okay again.

I only ever get the tiniest thing right—like the way Ms. Meyer's hair falls over her forehead when she corrects papers at her desk during English or the stretched-out shadow the windowpanes cast on the floor during math. That's enough, though. Sometimes.

My best work always seems to be when I draw dogs. I got the crooked back leg of a poodle just perfect one day and I nailed the snout and jaw of a Rottweiler even though he was running around the whole time I tried to draw him.

So I'm sitting near the dog run after school, drawing, when a guy in a crummy white SUV pulls up. He jumps out and opens the back door and five or six dogs tumble out and race to the dog run's gate. He slams the door shut and follows them.

I've seen him before. I recognize all the regulars. He's the only one who ever brings more than one or two dogs, though, and the weirdest thing is that he brings a different group all the time. I don't pay much attention to the people, though, not when there are so many dog ears and dog tails and so much dog fur to try to get just right.

I'm studying the dogs, then glancing down to try to catch the shapes and the colors and even the sounds of them with my pencil. I must be staring at the guy, or at least the dogs close to him, because he waves and heads over.

I've got my art gear spread out on the bench so I can't pack up and leave before he gets to me—I'm not what you call friendly to begin with and Erik has made it clear that most strangers are not safe for people like us.

But this guy's got a nice smile. Real. Not like some adults who smile with their mouth but not their eyes and not like the guys Erik has warned me about—bad, mean, sick people with no business talking to kids, who smile with just a little too much teeth showing.

This guy just looks like he's in some bubble of . . . clean. Crazy, I know, and nothing I've ever seen before. But it's there. I can see it in the way he jumps sideways to miss the Chihuahua who scampered in front of him and the way he laughs when the big mutt gooses him in the butt in that sniffy way dogs have.

"Hey," he says when he's finally standing in front of me. "I'm Greg; I've seen you drawing before. Can I take a look?"

Even though I've never shown anyone but Erik my sketches, I nod to the sketchbook closest to Greg. He picks it up and sits on the bench, but not too close, which makes me feel safe. He leans back and crosses his ankles as he turns each page.

"That's Neenie"—he points to a sketch of a terrier—"and this"—he flips to one of a pug—"is Gretchen."

I scan the dog park, looking for them. He catches my look. "They're not here today. Neenie got adopted day before yesterday and Gretchen was in a funk and stayed back to pout and think about what she did." He laughs at his own joke. I frown, not getting it. "Gretchen bit Slade today when I had them in the outdoor pen and so she lost her field-trip privileges until she can be better behaved."

I'm more confused than ever and he can tell. "I'm

Greg," he repeats, and puts out a hand for me to shake, and I do, slowly. "And I volunteer at the animal shelter over on Diehl. I bring a handful of the dogs over here to run after my shift. It's not really allowed"—he shrugs— "but what the powers that be don't know won't hurt them, and those guys deserve a better place to play than on concrete behind chain-link fences."

He's still carefully turning the pages of the sketchbook and nodding. "You've really captured their spirits. I don't know art, but I do know dogs, and this is really good."

"Thanks." I don't know what to say.

"What's your name?" he asks.

"Jamie."

"That's a good name for an artist—one name, like Christo, is memorable."

"I'm not an artist." Normally I don't like talking with someone I don't know, but the way he turns the pages and looks at the pictures and then back at the dogs makes me feel good.

"Sure you are. I'll prove it: What's the going price for your pieces?" My eyes open wide as he digs out his wallet. "I'm not kidding. I'll buy some. We put pictures of the dogs online along with descriptions to try to find them homes. But the photos, even if I do take most of them myself, are crap and don't do justice to the dogs. Not the way your drawings do. You could help them find homes."

Home.

He's asking me to help find homes for the dogs. Me.

"You could draw them in their pens, if you wanted. It must be kind of cold sitting on the bench."

I'm still thinking. Money. For my drawings. Homes. For the dogs, at least.

"Well, look," he says, pulling a few bills from his wallet. "Just think about it. Since you haven't named a price, I'm going to make you an offer: I'll give you five bucks each for the pictures of Gretchen"—*rrrrrip*, he carefully tugs her picture out of my sketchbook—"Simon, Papi and AJ." He gently tears out the other three pages and hands me a ten and two fives.

He looks so happy that I don't know what to say. Plus, I have twenty bucks in my hand.

"I've got to get the dogs back pretty soon. Come by the shelter someday—I'm usually there from three until six."

And then I hear a voice—mine—say, "Yeah, I think I will."

Greg drives off with the dogs and I sit looking at the twenty bucks.

I could buy four pizzas. I could even go to a grocery store and get . . . I don't actually know what I could get, Erik and I don't go to grocery stores so I'm not sure I'd know how to shop or what I'd do with the stuff when I got it.

Erik's Rule #4: Never own more than you can carry or stash in less than a minute and never stash anything you can't afford to lose.

Then I think about Erik's little notebook and his pouch of money and how worried he looks when he pulls either of them out. So I tuck the cash in my jeans pocket. Maybe Erik's not the only one in this family with an income now.

I don't want to tell Erik about the money until I make more and can help him with the apartment fund, but I can't keep this to myself.

So I go see Grandpa. His old folks' home is just a few blocks away from the dog park and I've got some time before I need to meet Erik back at Trudy's for the night.

Grandpa has always been the one fun and wonderful thing in our lives.

When we were little, he came over to get us one Sunday like usual and, well, he didn't like what he saw. He didn't say a word, just turned very white, and he picked up an empty paper bag from the liquor store that was on the floor and walked over and around the bodies sleeping it off, snoring, on the floor, and he gathered up anything that looked like it belonged to two kids. There wasn't much.

He took us away with him that day and we lived with him until two years ago and it was great. We ate frozen dinners together and watched sports on TV and he helped us with our homework and it was quiet and safe and clean. We had birthdays. Christmas. New clothes now and then. No one screamed and no one hit and nobody looked at you funny and tried to touch you in places and ways they shouldn't.

He used to take us on the weekends to see the guard

dogs at the junkyards down on Washington Avenue. Maybe that's where Erik learned how to make cheap fun. I don't know why we thought that was such a great way to spend a Sunday afternoon, to walk up and down that stretch of Washington where there were three or four junkyards and what we thought were huge and ferocious attack dogs, but I remember thinking we had the coolest grandpa in the world.

But then Grandpa got sick. Erik and I got home from school one day and overheard the neighbors talking about how Grandpa'd had a stroke and had been taken away in an ambulance. I didn't know what that meant, but Erik did.

"A blood vessel broke in Grandpa's head, Jamie. He's gone to the hospital for a while to get better. We have to keep a low profile until he's well enough to come back home, or Social Services will find out. We'll be taken away and put in foster homes, maybe separated. We can't have that."

"I'm scared."

"You never have to be scared when I'm around," he told me. "You just do what I say and everything will be fine. We have to pretend that someone, like from our family, is staying with us, though. People get weird about kids on their own. Don't let on we're alone, okay?"

Erik's the one person I could always trust, so I believed him.

We couldn't visit Grandpa in the hospital because we

were kids, but Erik made his voice low and pretended he was a grown-up and called every day to find out how Grandpa was doing. Grandpa couldn't talk, they said. For a couple of weeks we held things together at the apartment without him, eating canned food and setting the alarm clock so we wouldn't be late for school, while we waited for him to come back.

Grandpa never did come home, though. When he finally got released from the hospital, he was sent straight to the old folks' home.

Erik hung up the phone after he found out, and turned to me.

"Something broke in Grandpa's head when he had the stroke," Erik told me. "He's too confused to take care of himself."

"We could take care of him," I said. "We take care of each other."

Erik shook his head. "He's never going to get well enough to live with us again."

"We can live here by ourselves," I tried.

"They said the social worker from the care center is going to come and pack up Grandpa's things because he didn't have an emergency name in his medical records."

"But what about us? We live here too. They can't just kick us out."

"No one really knows we've been living with Grandpa, Jamie. It wasn't exactly official or legal. We don't want to call attention to ourselves because then Social Services will get involved."

"We don't want that."

"Right. So we've got to clear out."

We went back to the place we used to live.

We stayed for less than five minutes.

Nothing had changed since the day Grandpa took us away. The place was still full of empty bottles and loaded strangers. We saw a guy slap the woman who used to be our mother, holding her hair in one hand and yelling in her face about money.

But it was worth it because that's when Erik took the car. It was a piece of crap, he said, but no one would miss something this beat-up and the kind of people who hung out at the place we used to live wouldn't have insurance so nobody would come looking for it or get too upset that it was gone. He fixed it at the garage and it ran pretty good. Good enough for us.

We used to visit Grandpa every day. Erik said not to take it personally that Grandpa couldn't remember who we were.

"In his heart, he still knows us, Jamie, and we should act like he's still there. Just treat him like normal, even though he doesn't seem like the same person."

We only go once a week now, though. We bring him lemon drops and read the sports section to him. He might not know who we are, but we can tell that he likes to hear the baseball stats and football plays and basketball team lineups. The newspapers are usually old, from the waiting room on the first floor, but he doesn't notice and we don't care. We still like being with him, even if he doesn't know it's us.

I walk up the stairs to Grandpa's room on the fourth floor—I don't like to take the elevators because it creeps me out to be in a small place—and when I get to the door of his room, I can see that he's asleep.

I hate to say this, but I'm getting to like those visits best. The kind where I can just sit there in his quiet room and draw. Today I sketch Grandpa asleep in his bed. Well, actually, I just draw his hand resting on top of the blanket. I'm trying to draw his knuckles, which look so much bigger than the rest of his fingers, when I notice that he's got big ugly purple bruises on his wrists, just under the sleeves of his bathrobe.

I push back one sleeve and I see that he's got bruises that go all the way around his wrist. His skin is so papery and thin and the marks aren't just dark like when I get them, but black-purple-green-yellow and blotchy.

"Those are from the restraints." I turn to the voice from the door. It's Nan, the nicest of the aides who works on his floor. There's a lot of turnover at the place so we hardly ever know the people taking care of Grandpa. Which is good, Erik says, because if we don't know them, they don't know us, and that's how we like things.

"He got agitated the other day," Nan explained, "and we were worried he might fall out of bed in the night, so we put soft restraints on him to keep him safe."

I don't know what to say. What do you say when you find out someone has been tied down? I might know what to say, but I know I'm not going to tell Erik; it would just be one more thing for him to worry about.

Nan looks at me from the door, a little sad, I think. She knows that Erik and I are the only ones who visit Grandpa and she takes good care of him, she calls him "Mr. Dixon" and not just "dear" like some of the other staff do.

"Come with me," she says, and turns to leave the room.

I pat Grandpa's hand and start to say goodbye, but instead, I rip out the picture I'd been sketching of his hand and sign it, "From your grandson Jamie (the shorter one)." I prop it up on his bedside table so he'll see it when he wakes up. Then I turn and hustle after Nan, who's waiting for me by a food cart near the elevator.

"Here." She thrusts a paper bag at me. "These folks don't eat half their meals anyway. Take a couple of sandwiches and some pudding cups to share with that handsome brother of yours." She winks and pushes the cart down the hall before I can think of how to thank her.

I turn and head down the stairs, dinner in my hand and twenty bucks in my pocket. Other than finding out that Grandpa's getting worse, which I kind of already knew anyway even if I don't like to think about it much because there's nothing I can do to stop it, it's a pretty good day.

I jog-trot to Trudy's place because it's getting dark and I know Erik will be waiting for me by the outside door. We always go in and out of Trudy's place together so that we're not too much of a distraction to her. I don't know how you could distract someone who just sits in her bedroom watching TV and drinking beer all night after she gets home from work, but I do what Erik says.

I'm not going to tell him about the money I made yet and I'm definitely not going to bring up Grandpa's restraints, but I can't wait to show him that we're not eating leftover burgers tonight.

4

I love the library.

Every day after school I go there to do my homework. The library started out as another free fun place Erik found; we could go there and use their computers or slip into the big meeting room for programs where there's sometimes a plate of leftover cookies in the back.

I wish we could sleep in the library because it's warm and clean and I like the smell of books, but Erik says it's too risky to even try to hide out and crash there. Libraries are owned by the government and we do all we can to stay off that radar since we're kind of illegal—two minors living on their own and all. He won't even let me get a library card.

"You'd have to show proof of residency," he explained. "The school district might not realize our address is phony, but for sure a librarian would. They're sharp and they pay attention. We don't want them checking the address and figuring out we're not exactly what we say we are."

Erik's Rule #5: Stay off the grid, out of sight, out of the loop, don't do anything to call attention to yourself because the least little thing could trip you up.

Even though I don't have a library card, I borrow books anyway. I find a book, read as much as I can after I've gotten my homework done and then, until I've finished it, I stash the book in the natural science and mathematics section in the back corner. No one goes there much so it's safe. When I'm done reading the book, I put it back where I found it.

I have this trick I do to find the next book I'm going to read. I walk over to the stacks, close my eyes and reach for a book. It's nice to be surprised like that and I'm hardly ever disappointed in what I pick.

I'm done with my homework and I need a new book so I wander between the shelves until I find the right place. I never know where it's going to be, I just know that I keep moving until something tells me I'm where I'm supposed to be. Then I shut my eyes, reach out and take the first book I touch. I open my eyes, look down and see the words *Annie Oakley* on the cover above a picture of an old-fashioned woman with a pistol in her hand. There's something about her eyes that makes me want to open the book, even though I'm not really into history, and especially not history about girls and guns.

I take the book back to my seat, glance through it, and before I know it, I'm reading a biography of Annie Oakley. No, I'm not just reading, I'm sucked into the book in that great way where you lose track of time and you can't remember where you are and the words on the page are more real than what's around you.

Annie Oakley was a trick shooter in the eighteen hundreds, but that's not why I like reading about her. The part about Annie Oakley that really hit me was when I found out how she had such terrible foster parents that she called them wolves because they beat her and worked her nearly to death and, although the book didn't come right out and say it, probably hurt her in ways kids shouldn't be hurt.

Like me and Erik.

It's like being part of a club no one wants to join, but one where you can recognize the other people who belong because you know what it's like and, in ways you can't even explain, you understand each other.

But Annie Oakley didn't let that part of her life wreck her and she made something of herself later, when she got away, and she became rich and famous because of her shooting skill.

Even though it's crazy, even though she's been dead forever, I got the feeling that I would have liked Annie

Oakley. Drawing and shooting aren't anything like each other, but I kind of thought I knew what she must have felt like when she found out she was good at something that most other people aren't.

As I'm reading and wishing I'd gotten the chance to know Annie Oakley, I reach into my backpack to grab a sketchbook because I want to draw her. As I pull out the sketchbook, a flyer falls to the floor. Mrs. Fitzgerald handed them out in art class this afternoon, but I haven't read it.

It's an announcement for an art competition. Artists, singers, dancers, actors, writers and sculptors of any age and skill level can submit their work for a cash prize and an exhibition or performance during the month-long city culture fair. The top five winners will present their work at a reception.

Artists are supposed to submit a portfolio of fifteen to twenty-five pieces.

I can't help getting excited. Greg thought my drawings were good enough to get homes for the dogs, so maybe I have what it takes to enter the contest.

I flip through my sketches. I don't have anywhere near fifteen finished pieces. But the last day to enter is six weeks away and maybe that gives me enough time.

The pages are full of partial sketches and crossed-out attempts and I've hardly completed anything. But Greg recognized some of the dogs I've drawn. So I could probably work on finishing some works-in-progress, and do a few new ones.

I flip to a drawing of one of my favorites at the dog run—a spunky little corgi with the brightest, smartest look. If dogs had jobs, I just know this one would be a librarian dog.

I grab a pencil to finish this picture. I close my eyes, trying to remember exactly what the dog looked like so I can get it down on paper. I'm frustrated, though, because I can't imagine him clearly enough. I open my eyes and see the librarian at the circulation desk. He's got his head cocked the same way as the corgi at the park. I smile at myself, but I capture the tilt of the dog's head. Somehow, between what I already had on the page, what I remember and what I can see in the librarian, I get the angle and the shadows just right.

For the first time, I feel like a real artist.

We didn't work it out, officially, but Erik and I take turns having bad dreams about what it was like in the time before Grandpa took us away. Seems every few nights we wind up hugging in the dark with one of us going "Shhh, it's okay, I'm here, you're safe, it was only a dream, go back to sleep now." The only thing that changes is who's doing the shushing and who's shaking and sweating, sick to his stomach from the memories.

Erik's Rule #6: Stuff from the dark doesn't get talked about in the light. Ever.

Tonight, it's his turn to wake up and mine to do the shushing.

I'm still feeling smooth and even from my time at the library and I'm busy picturing drawings I want to make for the portfolio, so while he pulls himself together, I imagine the sketches I'm going to do. And I know that even if we don't talk about the memories in the night, I'm going to have to find a way to draw them.

We lie there awake for a while—no matter who has the dreams, neither of us can go back to sleep right away—and I remember that I've got to tell him about working at the shelter or he'll worry about where I am and what I'm doing.

"I'm going to start volunteering at the shelter in the afternoons. For the service hours requirement at school."

"Oh," he says, "that's nice. Dogs." His voice is getting sleepy and I can tell that pictures of the dog run are replacing whatever dreams woke us both up.

I think about my plan not to tell him I'm earning money drawing the dogs until I have a chunk of change I can show him. I can't decide if I want to impress him or surprise him. I don't think I've ever done either, so it's all good.

"I'm going with you the first day. You know that, right?" His voice isn't so sleepy and soft anymore now. He wants to make sure it's safe for me to be there.

"That's good," I say. "You'll like Greg; he's going to be my boss."

"How'd you meet him?"

"At the dog run."

"That's a good place."

"Yeah."

We must have fallen asleep because the next thing we know, it's morning and we can hear Trudy's alarm clock. We're always up and dressed and out the door before she's done hitting the snooze button for the sixth time.

I go to school, pay attention and keep to myself. All the while, I'm thinking about the shelter that afternoon and what I'll draw. It's hard to notice what's going on around me with so many ideas running through my mind.

Erik is waiting for me outside when I leave and I feel bad because I know he took off work to make sure I'm okay. He'll like Greg, though. I feel bad fibbing to Erik about the reason I'll be spending time at the shelter. He doesn't say anything on the drive over, but that's normal—Erik is almost as stingy about words as about money.

"Jamie. I'm glad you decided to take me up on my offer." Greg looks happy to see me as we walk through the front door. He's pinning descriptions of adoptable dogs to the bulletin board in the lobby.

"Uh, yeah, thanks, volunteering here will help with school. This is my brother, Erik." I'm speaking so fast it sounds like one really long word.

Greg is quick, though, or he has an older brother himself, because he doesn't miss a beat. "Good to meet you, Erik." He reaches out to shake hands. My brother is less friendly than I am, but even he reacts to Greg's basic good-guyness and says hello. He started looking around like he was trying to find something he might not like, but when he shakes Greg's hand, I notice that that squinty hard look he gets when he's sizing people up has disappeared.

"I've got to get to work," Erik says to me. "I'll see you later." Then he turns to Greg and nods. "Thanks for letting him work here."

"He's doing us the favor," Greg says. I try to think if anyone's ever said that about me, but I'm pretty sure this is a first.

Greg leads me through the door marked EMPLOYEES ONLY, and we go down a hallway and turn into a room filled with dogs. There's a concrete slab, like a mini-sidewalk, down the middle of the room, leading to a door. I can see an enclosed patio through the window. On either side of the little path are chain-link pens with doors.

The dogs all stand up when we come into the kennel, like they're really polite and want to show off their good manners. A few whine or bark at Greg, trying to get his attention, but they all wag their tails and push their noses through the holes in the fences, trying to reach us.

My throat tightens a little when I think that they're all hoping for someone to come save them from this place. Dogs weren't made to live in little concrete-floored chain-link pens. And it's wrong. Wrong in a way that I know is huge. I don't pray, but I find myself thinking, Please, please, please, hoping that people are on their way right now to take all these dogs out of here.

I think back to the running, barking, leaping, bounding, playing dogs in the dog park and how they all seem to react when their owner stands up from the bench he or she was sitting on. A few of the dogs make a game out of being caught and leashed so they can leave, but I've noticed that most of the dogs drop their game the very second their people start to move, and the dogs run to them, ready to leave their dog friends and dog games in an instant for their people lives.

Greg walks me down the aisle, pointing to each dog and introducing them all.

"This is Mac, he's an Irish setter. That's Gretchen, the pug you know from the park—you'll be happy to know she learned her lesson and hasn't snapped at anyone lately. Maya, the black Lab, is in this cage, and the dogs of indeterminate lineage are Topher, Buzz, Gib and Corky."

I let them all smell my hand through the fence and they seem to approve of me, because they all go back to lying down. A few curl up and sleep, the rest watch Greg and me talk.

"Don't go in the cages by yourself. You're not even supposed to be back here, so I can't imagine the trouble I'd get in if you got bitten or let one of the dogs escape."

"I'm just going to sit there and draw them." I'm already getting my sketchbook and pencils out of my backpack and deciding that I'm most interested in drawing the setter. I've never seen one in person before and I like the ripples in the fur on his flank.

I'm going to draw another four or five dogs today; that'll be twenty or twenty-five dollars, and I can't wait to put the money Greg will give me in my pocket with the first twenty bucks. I wonder how long this gig will last and how much money I can save up to give to Erik. I don't dare hope, but a tiny part of me wants to get going on the portfolio pieces I'm going to submit for the contest. The idea of the cash prize makes me dizzy.

Once I've drawn something, it's like it's burned in my mind, so even though I'll have to give Greg the original sketches of the dogs, I know I can draw them again for my portfolio.

I've never thought about what I was going to draw or had plans for what I would do next. I'm excited about the ideas I have and I can't wait to get to work.

But first I'm going to draw Greg. Mostly because I want a picture of him, but also because I need to see if I can capture the way his eyes seem to smile when he looks at the dogs. When he looks at me.

I don't spend much time looking in mirrors, but I'm pretty sure it's the same look on my face when I sit at the dog run and watch the dogs.

6

It's Saturday morning.

Erik works as many weekends as he can. He says days off weren't invented for people like us. Greg only volunteers at the shelter Monday through Friday so I can't go there. I'm not ready to find out if Grandpa still needs restraints. And now that I've been drawing at the shelter, up close and personal with the dogs and really getting to know them as individuals, I don't think I'd have as much fun at the dog park anymore.

So I head to the library. I'm going to sit in the comfy chair in the back corner near the restroom, put my feet up on the low windowsill and start working on the non-dog pictures for my portfolio.

I'd rather just submit twenty-five dog pictures, but

something tells me I need to show variety, and besides, I've got some other ideas I need to work on. Ever since the last time Erik had bad dreams, I've known what I have to draw.

The first sketch I start once I get settled in my chair comes from the place I never think about, and I'm surprised my pencil can take my hand where my mind would never go.

The memories make me run for the toilet, gagging. I knew that letting myself think about this would make me sick so I made sure I wasn't more than ten feet from the men's room. I vomit until there's nothing left inside me. Then I rinse my mouth out at the sink and head back to the chair, where I dropped my sketchbook.

I slash at the paper with my pencil, dark jagged lines, trying to figure out what screaming looks like—I know what it sounds like and I remember what it feels like, but I'm trying to put it on paper. I borrowed a box of pastels from the art room because I know this needs color. I slash some lines in acid green and bile yellow, smudging dirty gray shadows with the side of my pencil.

I remember the slaps and punches, the burns and the belts. Those I make fluorescent orange and bloodred, broken lines that dig into and across the page.

I can't do the rest.

Not yet.

Because my hands are shaking too much to keep going into that dark place in my head.

I will, though. Now that I've started, I know that I'll go back. That I'll find the colors and the shapes that will help me understand. Once I understand, then I'll be able to forget. Forget for real, not just pretend I can't remember.

Erik has never talked about that time or let me talk about it. But this picture I've drawn, well, I've said almost everything without saying a word.

It's only lines and colors, no clear people or objects, but it's just right and I know that anyone who looks at it will understand why Erik and I still wake up screaming sometimes.

The next one is Erik. Of course.

I draw him standing, looking off into the distance, with his shoulders back, and his profile looks like it belongs to a king or a god. I use golds, coppers, and bronzes so that he glows, warm and strong. I could never show this to him, it would make him embarrassed. But I know there's something real about it, something right. It's the exact opposite of the first picture and I know I'll put them back to back in my portfolio.

I draw another picture of Greg next, closing my eyes first to picture his little round glasses and his dark shaggy hair and the loose way he ambles, jeans riding low on his butt—he needs a good belt—and his T-shirt covered in dog hair. He's laughing as he watches the dogs and I can almost hear him, just from how I draw his face in warm greens and happy blues.

I've never used color before, I've always just sketched with soft pencils, and I'm surprised at how easily working with pastels comes to me and how much more I can see on the page.

I sketch the librarian. He's sitting at his desk across the room from me, answering someone's question, so I don't have to close my eyes like when I'm trying to get Erik and Greg. The librarian's face is serious, but content, like he's doing something terribly important, something he was meant to do, and like there's no place on earth he'd rather be than sitting here with piles of books around him. I go back to using my pencil and sketch him in black and white, like the print on a page, and I smile because it's the perfect, and only, way to catch who and what he is.

I can't help myself—I'm an artist who needs to know the names of his models. I pass by his desk like I'm on my way to the men's room and sneak a look at his name tag. ED S. I hurry back to my chair and sketch an ID pin.

I draw Grandpa, but not skinny and sick and tied to his bed like he is now. I remember the Grandpa from when I was little, leaning forward in his chair to watch a baseball game on TV, holding his breath to hear the call at first. I draw him wearing that plaid shirt that I didn't remember until I started drawing it. His wedding ring glints on his finger and there's a hint of shine on his bald head. I know it's not possible, but as I draw I swear I can smell the Ivory soap he used.

I sketch all day and I'm startled when the announcement comes over the intercom that the library will be closing soon. I page through the sketchbook, surprised at how much work I've done today.

Erik's Rule #7: Hard work is the only thing we can count on so we better get used to it.

I never thought I was any good.

I never wanted to show anybody my drawings.

But now I do.

Greg offers me a ride as we leave the shelter on Monday because it's raining. Even though showing him where I live is the last thing I want to do, he insists that he won't let me walk in the rain since we're leaving at the same time anyway.

My heart sinks when we get to Trudy's apartment building. Because I got a ride instead of walking, I'm early and Erik isn't home from work yet. That means I have to stand outside the building until he gets here—I'm not allowed to go into the places we stay if he's not with me. I don't mind hanging around, I do it every day, but something tells me that Greg isn't going to drive off and leave me standing in the rain.

"I, uh, forgot my key," I say, "so I'll just hang out at

the Laundromat across the street until my brother gets here."

"I've got nowhere to go, I don't work until later tonight, so I'll wait with you," he says.

"Oh, well, that's really nice," I say as I cross my fingers that Trudy will come home before Erik because I don't think Greg will buy it that we both forgot our keys. I look up and see that her apartment windows are dark and I feel a knot begin in my stomach.

This is why Erik and I try not to get too close to people—because you can't always keep them from knowing your business.

"You never asked what I do when I'm not at the shelter," Greg says.

I feel stupid for not having asked, which, I guess, he wanted me to do even though I think it's rude to put someone on the spot by asking them too many questions. He takes the pressure off me with his next sentence.

"You have really good manners not to pry, but I'll tell you anyway: I'm a drummer in a local band. The pay's not good, but it's a fun gig and gives me lots of free time in the day so I can work with the dogs."

"A drummer?"

"I was an investment banker for a bunch of years out of college. I made a fortune, but there was no joy to my life. I had lots of money but lots of problems."

"I'd love to have those kinds of problems."

He looks at me and says slowly, "Money isn't everything."

"It is if you don't have any."

"Ah."

We sit for a few seconds after that, each of us looking out the side windows.

"So it's just you and your brother?"

"No one knows that, though."

"That's what I thought." He drums his fingers on the steering wheel like he's hearing a song in his head and keeping the beat. "Do you really live here?"

"We're staying with a . . . friend. For a while."

"Then what?"

"Then we'll stay with someone else."

"Oh." He's still tapping his hands on the wheel.

"Rent is tough to swing, you know, just that first, last and deposit thing; we could handle rent, if it wasn't too much. Erik works hard. It's just . . ."

"Yeah, I know what you mean." He's still tapping and staring out the window and I get the feeling his mind is far away, but I'm not sure where, or if it was a mistake or a good thing to let him know so much about us. It's not something I've ever done before.

I'm glad to see Erik coming around the corner just then and I mumble goodbye and thanks and then slip out the door and slide into the shadows so that Erik doesn't see that Greg brought me home. Plus I'm anxious to get away from what I'm sure is pity and what I hope isn't the thought of calling someone to "help" us. Erik and I have worked really hard to keep far away from those things.

Erik is soaking wet from walking in the rain, but he doesn't seem to notice that I'm dry. He nods, I nod back and then we both take deep breaths and head into the building together.

We're on the fifth-floor landing when we hear thumping on the steps behind us. It's Greg, closing his cell phone.

"I found you a place," he says.

Erik looks at me and I know he's not happy. Before I can say anything, though, Greg starts talking again.

"It's a buddy's apartment. He joined the service and shipped out to basic training last week. He couldn't break the lease so I just called his sister, who's been keeping an eye on things for him. I asked if you could sublet and she said he'll be happy not to have to eat the rent as long as you don't trash the place. I told her you were friends of mine and I'd vouch for you. It's not much rent, because it's not much of a place. But it's clean and dry. It's just six months, though."

That's six months more than we've ever had before, I think. And it'll be ours. Mine and Erik's. And it's a start.

Erik's Rule #8: If it's even a little better than what came before, it's a lot better than what came before.

"Grab your stuff; we're out of here." That's what Erik always says to me when we're about to move, but this time Greg says it to both of us because we're just stand-ing there, frozen, on the fifth-floor landing.

"I can swing by his sister's place and get the key on the way over and you can give me the rent money and I can send my buddy's sister a check and she'll pay the super and no one will have to know the details. I'll see Jamie at the shelter, he can let me know everything's working out okay."

I hold my breath, thinking for sure Erik is going to say no, we're okay, we don't need help, but when I look over, he's not looking mad or uncomfortable, but tired and totally out of it.

"Okay," I say, breaking the silence and making the decision for us. We don't have to say anything to Trudy about moving out because I'm pretty sure we'd be doing this same grab-and-go routine in a few days anyway— we always get kicked out of the places we stay and she wasn't the friendliest person we ever knew to begin with.

Erik is still looking like he can't move and Greg is fiddling with his phone, and for a second I think Erik is just going to keep standing there, but he follows me down the stairs to our car and we wait for Greg to start his car and pull up in front of us.

Erik doesn't say anything as we drive, following Greg. We make a stop at a small house about ten blocks away and watch Greg jog to the door, get the key from the woman who answers his knock and then wave to us as he gets back in his car.

When we finally pull up in front of a shabby row of stores—a Mexican restaurant, a pawnshop, a convenience store and a secondhand shop—Greg gestures to us to park. Erik circles the block twice before a parking spot on the street by a liquor store opens up.

"C'mon." I grab our bags and my box of drawings. We walk to the doorway between the Mexican restaurant and the convenience store, where Greg is waiting for us.

"It's number five." He holds the key out to Erik. I don't think Erik is going to take it so I snatch it—I'm as hyper as Erik is out of it. I open my mouth to say thank you, but Greg's disappeared. *Poof,* like smoke, he's gone and it's just Erik and me and the key to our new place.

I shove the door open with my shoulder and, slowly, Erik follows me up a flight of narrow stairs.

We climb to the third floor and turn right at the landing. I squint at the numbers on the two doors in the dim hallway. I jerk my chin at the door on the left and say, "That's it."

I turn to Erik, hand him the key and feel the stab of surprise run through him as I place it in his hand.

Because we've never had a key to any place we've ever stayed. We usually have to wait in the apartment hallway or sit in the car on the street waiting for whoever we're crashing with to come home if they don't answer our knock. And Grandpa was always waiting for us to get home.

We're standing at the door and I'm wondering why he's not unlocking it already and I look down and see that his hand is shaking. Erik's hand is shaking as he lifts the key to the lock and he's moving like he's under-water or in a dream and I take a deep breath and then I realize that I'm shaking too, and finally he opens the door and we stand there and look.

We can see the entire place from the doorway. It's a furnished studio, small and grubby and painted hot pink. Every wall. I see a door that leads to what must be a bathroom. There's a futon and a ratty couch and a dinged-up dresser and some cinder blocks and boards making a little bookcase and a tiny table and two mis-matched kitchen chairs. The kitchen is a corner of the room with a small fridge and a two-burner stove and a mini-oven.

A stove and an oven.

We can heat up the burgers Erik brings home for supper. We can have hot food.

We don't have to sleep on the floor and we don't have to share a bathroom with other people and we can take our things out of our duffel bags for the first time in more than two years and we aren't going to come back someday to find our stuff outside the door, which means it's time for us to move on.

I feel dizzy and lean against the door frame. I notice that Erik has put his hand against the wall to steady himself, too.

We have a place.

After all this time and thinking it would never happen for us, *boom,* we're shutting the door behind us and flipping the lock.

Neither of us has cried in a really long time and we've sure never cried from relief.

But tonight, we come close.

I'm sitting against the wall at the end of the row of kennels, trying to get the ear right on a golden retriever who's sleeping, tucked in a little dog ball in the pen to my right, when I hear a gacking sound.

I look up from my sketchbook and see the Border collie two pens over. She's standing with her legs spread, head down, heaving. A shiver passes through her body and she starts to shake.

She takes a couple of steps forward and flops to the ground, her legs useless and her balance gone. I jump up and rush over, ignoring the rule not to enter any dog's area without supervision.

By the time I get to her pen, she's lying on her side, twitching and heaving, spasms racking her entire body, her face jerking in her own vomit. I fumble with the latch on the gate and see that she's lying in a puddle of pee. I throw the door open and drop to my knees next to her.

"Shhh, it's okay, I'm here, you're safe." I automatically mumble the words I always say to Erik when he has bad dreams as I reach out to touch her flank, letting her know she isn't alone.

Erik's Rule #9: Everything is less scary when you're not alone.

Her body is jerking and her legs are pedaling as if she's trying to run away from whatever has taken over her body. Her eyes are open but unfocused, and she snorts, trying to breathe, arching and bucking on the concrete in her own filth.

I feel cold and numb, like I might vomit or wet myself, too. I want to make whatever this was stop because she looks terrified and I'm sick to my stomach, hoping she isn't in pain.

As I stroke her fur and murmur soft words, she gradually settles down, her legs stop thrashing and her breathing quiets. Her eyes close, and other than the frantic pounding of her heart, which I can feel through the side of her chest, I can tell she's getting calm.

I keep petting her and talking to her, nonsense about what a good dog she is and how pretty her coat is and what a beautiful line there is to her head and how much I want to draw her when she feels better.

Her heart slows down to a normal pace and she stops panting and flailing. Her eyes flutter and she gives one last shudder and seems to move from whatever was happening to her into a kind of sleep. I ignore the stench of her puke and the fact that I'm kneeling in urine and I never stop petting her and talking softly.

A few minutes later, her eyes flutter open and she jerks, scrambling to sit up. She's weak, though, or dizzy, and she starts to tip over. I reach out to grab her so she doesn't fall to the ground, and I pull her into my lap. I wipe away the sticky trickle of spitty throw-up that clings to the side of her muzzle. She looks up at me, surprised, I think, seems to sigh and rests her chin on my arm as I cradle her in my lap. I rock her back and forth gently, somehow feeling the warmth and strength flow back to her.

She pulls away finally, as if she were just waking up, and turns her face to me, that bright Border collie look back in her eyes, and I can feel her tail start to whip back and forth. She tries to scooch around in my lap so she can kiss my face—the rank smell of her pukey breath makes me want to turn away, but I don't—and I hear the door of the kennel open.

"What are you doing in the pen?"

I look up at Greg entering the room with a mop and a bucket.

"Something bad happened to this one," I say. "She

threw up and peed and then fell down and started shaking all over."

"Oh, yeah, poor girl. She's old and has seizures. The owner didn't want to deal with the hassle and mess." Greg kneels next to us, as if he doesn't notice the smell of puke and piss. And maybe he doesn't. "She's a good soul, this one."

"Why does she have seizures?"

"The vet says it's just one of those things, he can't find anything wrong with her. She doesn't have them all the time."

"Do they hurt her? Is she scared?"

He smiles as she shimmies around in my lap so she can nuzzle my ears. "You wouldn't think so by looking at her, would you?"

"What's going to happen to her?"

"She probably won't be adopted." He shakes his head. "Most people don't want to take on the responsibilities of an older dog who's hard of hearing, with bad eyesight, and has seizures."

"So then she'll just live here forever? In this pen?" Even the Toyota was better than this dog prison, I think. Because at least Erik and I had each other.

"It's not that bad," Greg says. "We do the best we can. It's a no-kill facility so she'll live out her life and be warm and clean and looked after and she'll always have enough to eat."

"Oh . . ." I look down at her. The seizure must have

made her tired, because she's starting to doze in my arms. Her weight and heat feel good and my eyes sting to think of her alone in the dark, falling down with no one to hold her and talk to her until she feels more like herself. I blink away the tears that spring to my eyes and bury my face in her neck. She sighs again.

Greg looks at me, looks down at the Border collie sleeping in my lap, over at the door leading to the outside pen and then back at us. "Why don't you just take her outside for some fresh air? I have to clean up this mess. She's new, only been here a couple days, you know. I haven't even entered her paperwork into the system. It's kind of like no one but you and I know she's here."

I look up at him and he winks, leans down to pet the collie goodbye and walks away.

And, just like that, I have a dog.

And the dog has me.

Erik is smiling.

I must have fallen asleep after I brought my dog back to our place—she was curled up next to me on the futon, tucking her back between my butt and knees—because I open my eyes and see Erik standing over us, looking down.

Smiling.

And when I see his face, I realize I can't remember the last time I've seen him smile.

"I got a dog, Erik."

"I see that."

"I've been making money. Sketching. I draw pictures of the dogs at the shelter and Greg pays me for them and puts them on a website. They help the dogs find a home because Greg says I capture their spirit, and, well, this one, even though she's got a great spirit and is a wonderful person, I mean dog, isn't the kind who's going to find a good home if we don't take her."

Erik just looks at us.

"I'll take care of her and feed her and clean up after her and the floor is linoleum so she won't ruin anything. And she's real old and housebroken so she won't bark or be a nuisance."

"She's real nice, Jamie, but I don't know how we can keep her."

"We can't get rid of Annie Oakley."

"What?"

"That's what I named her. I read a book about Annie Oakley, she was a trick shooter a long time ago and she, well, I don't suppose she talked much about the part that happened before, either."

"Oh."

"And we can't send her back to the shelter. Someone already did that, and, well, no one will want her because she's old and deaf and has seizures, but I don't mind."

I wait, nervous and sweating and wondering if he'll agree to another mouth to feed and more worries. He's probably worried too that there might be rules about not having pets, and worried about the mess she might make. But this doesn't seem like the kind of place that would be real strict, because it's not fancy. And Greg thought it was okay for me to bring her here. I know I shouldn't push Erik, but I can't lose Annie Oakley.

Erik's Rule #10: If you have to know now, the answer is no; if you can wait a while, we'll see.

I hope he just says yes right this very second.

Erik studies Annie Oakley for a little while. Then he sighs and shrugs. "This family could use a good woman. Welcome home, Annie Oakley."

Her tail thumps on the bed like she knows exactly what he means.

Erik flops next to me on the futon. "Shove over and make some room."

I do and Annie Oakley stretches out, her rump against me and her chin resting on Erik's arm.

And I know that tonight, at least, no one's going to have bad dreams or seizures.

10

Family.

Erik called us a family last night when he said we could keep Annie Oakley.

And he said *home,* too.

I've never heard Erik say those words.

I lie awake all night. Not like I usually do, wondering where we're going next or trying to think of anything but the reason Erik or I woke up. Tonight I'm thinking about family and home and art.

I get up off the futon. Annie Oakley wakes up and watches me go to my backpack to get my sketchbook and pencils and take them to the bathroom where I can turn on the light but not wake up Erik. As I shut the door, I see her creep over to sleep with him.

I sit with my back to the tub, my sketchbook on my lap.

Although I just caught a glimpse as she settled herself next to him, I draw Annie Oakley and Erik sleeping, curled up together on the futon.

When I'm done, I look over the finished drawings in my cardboard folder, pulling out the ones that don't need any more work—the colored one about what came before, Erik, two of Greg, the librarian at his desk, Grandpa watching baseball, Erik and Annie Oakley sleeping, and the best of the dogs from the shelter and the dog run.

When I count them, I'm surprised to see that I have fifteen. The exact number I need. Before I can chicken out, I slip into my clothes, and at the door to the hallway, I snap my fingers for Annie Oakley. She leaps off the futon and pads over to me. I clip the leash onto her collar and close the door behind us silently.

It's early, six or six-thirty, and we head to the library. I know it's still closed, but there's an after-hours drop box where I can leave my portfolio. The entry form says any government building will accept submissions.

I've been carrying the form around. I pull it out of my backpack when we get to the library and I sit on the steps filling it out. I feel a zingy thrill when I write down our address. Then I slip the form into the folder with my work and put the whole thing in the drop box.

I can't possibly win. But in the end I'm submitting

my work because the contest gave me a reason to draw all the things I'll never be able to talk about.

I know Erik is still worried. He stresses about the money pouch and the expense notebook, and now he has a little calendar, too, in which he counts the days until our six-month sublet is up and we have to find a new place. And Grandpa is never going to get better and remember us.

So things aren't perfect.

But for today, the sun is coming up and my fifteen finished drawings are in the drop box and Annie Oakley stands next to me, leaning into my leg, and we're going home to see Erik.

Erik's Rule #11: Good enough is enough for us.

ABOUT THE AUTHOR

Gary Paulsen is the distinguished author of many critically acclaimed books for young people, including three Newbery Honor Books: *The Winter Room, Hatchet,* and *Dogsong.* He won the Margaret A. Edwards Award given by the ALA for his lifetime achievement in young adult literature. Among his Random House books are *Flat Broke; Liar, Liar; Masters of Disaster; Woods Runner; Lawn Boy; Lawn Boy Returns; Notes from the Dog; Mudshark; The Legend of Bass Reeves; The Amazing Life of Birds; The Time Hackers; Molly McGinty Has a Really Good Day; The Quilt* (a companion to *Alida's Song* and *The Cookcamp*)*; How Angel Peterson Got His Name; Guts: The True Stories Behind* Hatchet *and the Brian Books; The Beet Fields; Soldier's Heart; Brian's Return, Brian's Winter,* and *Brian's Hunt* (companions to *Hatchet*)*; Father Water, Mother Woods;* and five books about Francis Tucket's adventures in the Old West. Gary Paulsen has also published fiction and nonfiction for adults. His wife, Ruth Wright Paulsen, is an artist who has illustrated several of his books. He divides his time between his home in Alaska, his ranch in New Mexico, and his sailboat on the Pacific Ocean. You can visit him on the Web at GaryPaulsen.com.

Gary Paulsen is available for select readings and lectures. To inquire about a possible appearance, please contact the Random House Speakers Bureau at rhspeakers@randomhouse.com.